Trapped

Trapped

Peg Kehret
and Pete the Cat

DUTTON CHILDREN'S BOOKS

DUTTON CHILDREN'S BOOKS
A division of Penguin Young Readers Group

Published by the Penguin Group
Penguin Group (USA) Inc., 375 Hudson Street, New York, New York 10014, U.S.A. •
Penguin Group (Canada), 90 Eglinton Avenue East, Suite 700, Toronto, Ontario,
Canada M4P 2Y3 (a division of Pearson Penguin Canada Inc.) • Penguin Books Ltd,
80 Strand, London WC2R 0RL, England • Penguin Ireland, 25 St Stephen's Green,
Dublin 2, Ireland (a division of Penguin Books Ltd) • Penguin Group (Australia),
250 Camberwell Road, Camberwell, Victoria 3124, Australia (a division of Pearson
Australia Group Pty Ltd) • Penguin Books India Pvt Ltd, 11 Community Centre,
Panchsheel Park, New Delhi - 110 017, India • Penguin Group (NZ), Cnr Airborne
and Rosedale Roads, Albany, Auckland 1310, New Zealand (a division of Pearson New
Zealand Ltd) • Penguin Books (South Africa) (Pty) Ltd, 24 Sturdee Avenue, Rose-
bank, Johannesburg 2196, South Africa • Penguin Books Ltd, Registered Offices:
80 Strand, London WC2R 0RL, England

Library of Congress Cataloging-in-Publication Data
Kehret, Peg.
Trapped! / Peg Kehret and Pete the Cat.—1st ed.
p. cm.
Summary: When his owner, Alex, finds an illegal animal trap in the woods, Pete the
cat faces grave danger as he tries to help his human friends find the culprit who set
the trap.
ISBN 0-525-47728-4 (hardcover)
[1. Trapping—Fiction. 2. Cats—Fiction.] I. Title.
PZ7.K2518Tra 2006
[Fic]—dc22
2005032962

Published in the United States by Dutton Children's Books,
a division of Penguin Young Readers Group
345 Hudson Street, New York, New York 10014
www.penguin.com/youngreaders
Printed in USA • First Edition
1 2 3 4 5 6 7 8 9 10

For Rosanne Lauer,
my editor and friend for twenty years
—P.K.

For all the shelters that help stray cats
—PETE

Trapped

Prologue

I am Pete the cat, co-author of this book. For some reason, my publisher thinks there should be a note here at the beginning to explain why a cat has written a book. If you ask me, no explanation is necessary, but nobody asked me. People never do. The humans think they are the ones in charge; we cats know better.

This is the third book that my person, Peg, and I have written together, and we used the same format as before. My parts are in italics; hers are not. In case you haven't read them, the other two books are THE STRANGER NEXT DOOR and SPY CAT. Peg says it's shameless to promote the first two books by listing them here, but I say if you haven't read them you've missed out on some good reading, and I'm only doing you a favor.

There is a fine cat hero in all three books. He is clever, courageous, and capable. If you want to describe him, remember the three C's. He's also exceptionally handsome. His name is Pete.

I told Pete that characters in novels are not supposed to be real, but he insists there's no need to make up a pretend cat when the perfect feline is willing to be in the story. When I suggested he could add a fourth C—corpulent— to his description, he hissed and left the room.

Pete IS a highly unusual cat. I chose him at the humane society because his papers said "good with children." I wanted a cat who would enjoy having my grandchildren come to visit. The papers didn't mention literary talent, so I had no idea that I was adopting a cat who could read and write.

I can talk, too, but she hasn't yet learned to understand me. Humans are not as bright as cats are.

One day when I was working on a new book, I left my computer unattended for a few minutes. When I returned, I saw that half a page had been added to my story. The new part was signed: "by Pete the Cat."

At first I thought my husband had played a joke on me; then I remembered that Carl had gone to the hardware store. No one was home except my dog, Lucy, who was asleep on her pillow, my other cat, Molly, who was napping in her heated bed, and Pete, who was watching me from the other end of the library table that I use for a desk.

No, I thought. Pete couldn't have written this. It's impossible!

Ha! That proves you should not jump to conclusions. I

not only wrote that section, but from then on I wrote two or three pages every night while Peg was asleep.

It's true. I began leaving the computer on at night, and when I'd get up in the morning, there would be new pages in the book, written from the cat's point of view. Someone had changed the villain from an escaped convict to a pit bull, and someone had written new parts of the story. Of course, I never actually SAW Pete typing on the keyboard, but what other explanation is there? Everyone else in my family stays in bed all night; Pete's the one who always prowls around in the dark.

You don't SEE lots of things that are real: electricity, cell-phone signals, cats reading newspapers. I learned to read at the humane society, where a copy of the Wall Street Journal *got put on the floor of my kennel every morning. The staff used that paper because the ink in the newsprint doesn't smear off onto cat fur the way other papers do. I would have preferred to read CAT FANCY magazine, but I learned a lot from the* Wall Street Journal.

Once I realized how quickly I could write a book with Pete's assistance, I was happy for his help. Writing is hard work, so it was wonderful to get up every morning and discover that the current book was two or three pages longer than when I went to bed. Aside from the pit bull, the only parts I had to change were the lines where Pete described himself as lean or slender. Anybody with eyes can see that

Pete is—as my veterinarian tactfully put it—"a bit on the pudgy side."

What does he know? Anyone who would stick a thermometer up a cat's rear end is not to be trusted.

Now that you know how we came to collaborate, I hope you'll enjoy the book that Pete and I wrote together.

Books. Plural. All of the books I wrote are good. Of course, the byline on all three books should say, "By Pete the Cat, with a little help from Peg Kehret." I did most of the work.

1

Alex found the trap by accident.

He and his best friend, Rocky, were in the woods, searching for deer antlers. The undergrowth in this part of the woods was thick, making it hard to walk. An hour into their hike, Alex stopped to take a drink from his water bottle. He wiped his brow on his shirtsleeve, his eyes scanning the area around him.

"I'm starting to think it's an urban legend that deer shed their antlers," Rocky said. "If it were true, we would have found some by now."

"Dad swears it's true," Alex said. "He says if I keep looking, I'll find some antlers. When I do, I'm going to mount them and hang them on my bedroom wall."

"Not me," Rocky said. "I'm going to sell mine on eBay."

"Right. After we knock ourselves out looking for them, you don't plan to keep them." Rocky's mom had started a home business selling items for people on eBay; now Rocky kept threatening to sell something good, such as his Game Boy or his bike, but he never did it.

As Alex screwed the top back on the water bottle, he noticed a piece of metal on the forest floor ahead of him, caught in the shaft of sunlight that filtered through the trees.

"Look over there," Alex said. "What's that?"

Rocky came closer and looked where Alex was pointing. Both boys walked toward the rusty metal.

"It's a trap!" Alex said. "An animal trap."

"It's set," Rocky said. "Look. There's a piece of meat in it."

The boys looked down at the strong steel trap, which was tucked between a huckleberry bush and a clump of salal. Flies buzzed around a piece of raw meat being used as bait.

Alex gulped. "I hate to think what that trap would do to the foot of an animal that steps on it," he said.

"Is trapping still legal?" Rocky asked.

"I don't know. If it is, it shouldn't be. That thing looks cruel, to me."

"Let's set it off," Rocky said, "so it can't hurt an animal."

Alex found a sturdy branch, about two inches in diameter, that had blown to the ground. He poked the broken end of the branch into the trap until it touched the bait. Instantly, the two pieces of steel snapped shut, breaking the branch in half.

Alex jumped back. He looked at the piece of branch that was still in his hand. "I'm glad that branch wasn't the leg of a fox or a coyote," he said.

"Or a dog. What if we had brought Rufus with us?" The boys often took Rocky's dog along when they went exploring, even though Rufus had only three legs. Since they had planned to hike farther than usual that day, they had left him home.

"Be careful walking out of here," Alex said. "There may be more than one trap."

Alex didn't want to hunt for antlers any longer. The trap made the woods seem unsafe, and frightening. He could tell that Rocky was ready to go home, too. They didn't even have to discuss it; they both just turned back the way they had come.

After the boys retraced their path out of the woods, they hurried down the road toward home.

When they turned the corner onto Valley View Drive, Alex's younger brother, Benjie, waved at them from his "spy station" on the empty lot at the end of the block.

"I saw you coming," Benjie called. "I was using my binoculars to watch for flying green panthers, and I saw you instead. Did you find any antlers?"

"No, but we found a trap."

Benjie's eyes widened. "What kind of trap? A bear trap? Was there a bear in it? Did he growl and try to get out?"

"There wasn't a bear," Alex said, "but there was meat in

it, for bait. We used a big stick to make the trap go off so it won't snap shut on an animal."

Benjie quickly gathered his spy kit and binoculars and went home with Alex and Rocky. Mr. and Mrs. Kendrill were sitting at the kitchen table with their checkbook, paying bills, when the boys arrived.

Alex's big white-and-brown cat, Pete, sat on the window ledge, watching the birds at the feeder. He jumped down and hid behind the couch when he heard Benjie's footsteps pound across the porch. When Benjie was excited, which was often, he talked loudly and moved fast; Pete preferred to watch and listen from a safe place.

Benjie rushed inside first. "Alex and Rocky found a humongous trap in the woods," he said, "and they set it off with a big stick. I bet somebody's trying to catch one of the flying green panthers so they can sell it to a circus."

"What kind of trap?" Mrs. Kendrill asked.

"It was made of steel bands," Alex said, "with a piece of meat inside. When we poked the stick at the meat, the trap clamped shut."

"It's a cat trap!" Pete said. "I've heard of those. The humans who set them always claim they're trying to catch coyotes or skunks, but the truth is they trap a lot of cats that way, including pet house cats. They catch dogs, too." His tail swished angrily back and forth.

"It was wicked-looking," Rocky said. "It would do some serious damage to any animal that stepped in it."

"That sounds to me like one of those leghold traps," Mr. Kendrill said. "They aren't legal in this state anymore. There was an initiative on the ballot a few years back, and the public voted to outlaw leghold traps. Since then, there have been a few attempts at getting the state legislature to reinstate them, but, as far as I know, it hasn't happened."

"*I should hope not,*" Pete said. "*If cats could vote, those traps would not be legal, that's for sure. Of course, if cats could vote, a lot of things would be better.*"

"If that kind of trap isn't legal," Mrs. Kendrill said, "maybe we should report this to the sheriff."

"Or the game warden," Mr. Kendrill said. "Do you boys know exactly where the trap was? Could you find it again?"

Alex and Rocky looked at each other. "It was way out in the woods," Alex said, "but I think we could find it."

"*This is one more reason why cats are superior to humans,*" Pete said. "*Cats never set traps—not even mousetraps. Cats never cheat or tell lies, either.*"

"I think there's a Department of Fish and Wildlife that handles matters like this," Mr. Kendrill said.

"*Is there a Department of Cats?*" Pete asked. "*Why should the fish and wildlife get their own government agency? Cats are more deserving of representation than trout or moose. Who decides these things? Probably the humans, who know the least about animals. Now if cats were in charge. . . .*"

"Alex," Mrs. Kendrill said, "did you forget to feed Pete this morning? I can't think with all that meowing."

"I'm not meowing," Pete said. "I'm expressing my opinion about a serious matter." It was exasperating. He could understand everything the humans said, but they had not yet learned to understand him. The only good part of the situation was that when he talked, they usually thought he was begging for food, which got his bowl refilled more often than it would be otherwise.

"I fed him," Alex said. "I think he's excited because he can tell we're upset." He picked up Pete and stroked his fur.

"Lizzy isn't meowing," Benjie said.

Pete looked sadly at the black-and-tan-striped kitten that the Kendrills had adopted. It was one of the great disappointments of his life that Lizzy could only speak and understand Cat. Pete had tried to teach her what the humans were saying, but she had never caught on. She didn't know how to read, either.

It would be terrible, Pete thought, to go through life unable to read a book or a newspaper. Lizzy couldn't even look up words in the dictionary, which was one of Pete's favorite pastimes. Pete was especially fond of words that began with the letters c-a-t. But Lizzy spent her days happily playing with catnip toys and napping in her basket, unaware of what she was missing.

"Let's tell Mrs. Sunburg what sort of trap you found and ask her advice," Mrs. Kendrill suggested. "She'll probably know who to call."

Pete purred, and snuggled close to Alex. He liked Mrs. Sunburg and her granddaughter, Mary, who lived next door. They were foster parents for an animal rescue group, and they always kept freeze-dried salmon treats on hand for visiting cats.

"Good idea. We'll go talk to her right now." Alex put Pete down, then headed for the door with Rocky right behind him.

"Wait for me," said Benjie, who had one hand in the cookie jar. He quickly removed two snickerdoodles.

"I'll go with you," Mr. Kendrill said. "I want to hear what she thinks."

"So do I," Mrs. Kendrill said. "I don't like the idea of you boys finding that trap. One of you could have stepped in it! And who knows how many more of them there are."

When his family went out the door to head toward the neighbors' house, Pete slipped out, too, and followed them across the grass. He wanted to hear what Mrs. Sunburg had to say about trapping. A well-informed cat, Pete thought, is a safer cat.

2

Alex and Rocky described what they'd found, and drew a sketch of it.

"That's a leghold trap," Mrs. Sunburg said. "They're horrible. They clamp down on the animal's leg and then—well, you don't want to hear the details. It makes me sick to think about it."

"Is that kind of trap legal?" Alex asked.

"Not in this state. The voters outlawed them three years ago. It was about time, if you ask me. More than eighty other countries around the world have banned leghold traps entirely."

"Either someone doesn't know the traps are illegal, or they figure they'll never get caught," Mary said.

"I don't think it's legal to trap at this time of year, regardless of what kind of trap is used," Mrs. Sunburg said. "Can you find the trap again?"

"Yes," Rocky replied.

"Good. I'll call Eric and report this."

"Eric?" Mr. Kendrill said.

"Eric Rogers. He's a licensed humane officer, which means he has the authority to make arrests and issue citations. I know him through the wildlife rehabilitation center." She went to her desk, looked up the number, and called.

"Trapping season ended March 31," she said, after she hung up. "He'll try to get here tomorrow afternoon, to take a look. He said all traps are supposed to have an identification tag with either a state ID number or the trapper's name and address."

"I didn't see a tag," Alex said.

"Neither did I," said Rocky, "but we weren't looking for one."

Mrs. Sunburg said, "Eric told me if there's no tag, it's hard to catch a trapper. Unless you see him setting or emptying the traps, or find him selling fresh pelts, it's hard to prosecute."

Pete's tail flipped from side to side when he heard the words "fresh pelts."

"We could spy on him," Benjie said. "We could sit in the woods near the trap and wait for him to come, and then take pictures of him setting the trap."

"You'll do no such thing," Mrs. Kendrill said. "I don't want you boys watching that trap. It's too dangerous."

"Keep Pete inside, too," Mr. Kendrill said. "He doesn't have enough sense to stay out of the woods, and a trap like that would kill him."

"It wouldn't kill a flying green panther," Benjie said. "They're so strong, they'd bite right through the trap and then they'd fly away." He snapped his teeth together several times, while he flapped his arms like wings and ran in circles.

"Thanks for your help," Mr. Kendrill told Mrs. Sunburg. "We knew we should report the trap, but we didn't know who to call."

Pete followed his family home. It took all his willpower to remain quiet. He wanted to protest against Mr. Kendrill's mistaken remark that Pete didn't have enough sense to stay out of the woods. Pete knew he had plenty of sense, more than the humans, in fact, but he didn't want to call attention to himself.

The Kendrills had decided that Pete and Lizzy should stay indoors, so Pete had to be cautious about sneaking out. Alex and Benjie sometimes ignored him when he dashed out the door, but Mr. and Mrs. Kendrill were strict about trying to keep him inside.

Lizzy didn't mind being an indoor cat, but Pete was unable to control his curiosity about what happened beyond his own front door. How could he guard his family and be an effective watch cat if all he did was nap on the rug?

When his people went inside, Pete slid quietly in the door with them.

The next morning, Rocky, Alex, and Mary met after breakfast to plan their day.

"I think we should hike back into the woods where we were yesterday," Alex said, "and find the trap, and see if it has an ID tag."

"Your mother said you couldn't go back there," Mary said.

"She said not to go back and watch the trap. We aren't going to watch it; we'll only go close enough to be sure we can find it again, and to look for an ID."

Mary raised her eyebrows and gave Alex the kind of look his mother gave him when she knew he was trying to get away with something.

"What if the trapper has moved it?" Rocky said. "If he found the trap set off, with no animal caught, he might have moved it to a different place."

"All the more reason why you should not be tromping around up there," Mary said. "What if it has been moved, and you don't see it? What if one of you steps in it?"

"We'll be careful," Rocky said.

"You don't have to come," Alex said.

Mary looked from Alex to Rocky. "If you two are going, I'm going, too," she said. "You might need me to run home and call 911 when your foot is stuck in a trap."

"Let's get started," Alex said.

"What are you going to tell your parents?" Mary asked.

"I don't have to tell them anything. They left a little while ago with a list of errands that should take them all morning. By the time they get back, we'll be home. They knew Rocky and I were going to hang out together this morning."

Mary rolled her eyes. Then she went home, told her grandma that she was going on a hike with Alex and Rocky, got a bottle of water, and rejoined the boys at Alex's house. She found them in the kitchen, looking dismayed. Benjie was there, too, wearing his spy badge.

"I thought you went with Mom and Dad," Alex said.

"I didn't want to go. It's boring at the grocery store and all those other places. They said I could stay with you. I'm going to sit in my spy station and watch the cars that go past. Maybe I'll see something suspicious."

Alex hesitated. He knew he couldn't leave Benjie here by himself, but he didn't want to take his brother along, either.

"What are you guys going to do?" Benjie asked.

"We were planning to hike up the hill," Alex said.

"To the trap?"

"We want to be sure we know where we left the road and headed into the woods, so we can take Eric to the right place when he comes."

"I'll go with you," Benjie said. "That'll be more exciting than watching cars. Maybe there'll be a bear in the trap this time or a rhinoceros."

"If you come along, you have to stay with me," Alex said. "No running ahead or lagging behind."

"Okay." Benjie lifted the cookie-jar lid. "If we're going far, we'd better have a snack with us," he said as he took eight chocolate-chip cookies, dropped them in a plastic bag, and added the bag to the backpack he called his spy kit.

"I'll go, too," Pete said. "Cats have a keen sense of smell, to say nothing of our superior intelligence. If there are traps in those woods, I'll lead you to them."

"What if we find another trap?" Benjie asked.

"Then we'll make a note of where it is and report it."

"If I see that trapper, I'll shred his pant leg and bite him in the ankle," Pete said. He went to his scratching post and began sharpening his claws.

"Let's go," Alex said. He opened the door, then pushed in on the lock button so it would lock behind them when it closed.

Pete dashed toward the open door, but Alex saw him coming and stuck his foot out to block Pete's path. Then he scooped up the cat and held him while Rocky, Mary, and Benjie went out.

"Put me down!" Pete yelled. "You're making a big mistake

if you don't take me along. I can smell better than you can, and hear better."

"I'm sorry, Pete," Alex said. "You and Lizzy have to stay inside."

"I'm a spy cat. I'll look for hidden traps, and I'll protect you from danger."

Alex stepped out the door, still holding Pete. Then he pulled the door almost all the way shut, set Pete on the floor inside, and quickly closed the door before Pete could turn around.

"You're making a categorical mistake," Pete said. "If you have a catastrophe, I won't be there to help you."

Pete had spent an hour that morning reading the dictionary and practicing words that began with the letters c-a-t. He was glad for a chance to use these new words, even though nobody was listening.

He jumped on the window ledge and watched the four children go down the driveway and turn onto Elm Lane. Then he headed for his food bowl, glad to see that Alex had remembered to fill it with crunchies that morning.

If you can't have what you want, Pete thought, you can always console yourself with a little snack.

To reach the wooded area where they'd found the trap, the kids first needed to hike up the winding, rural road on the far side of their housing development. They set off, with

Rocky and Mary in the lead, and Alex and Benjie close behind.

They passed the small community of Hilltop, where the paved road ended, and continued up the gravel road. Thick stands of trees bordered both sides of the road, making it seem as if they were far out in the wilderness instead of only about two miles from home. According to the county map, most of this land was owned by a large wood-products corporation, with a few private plots here and there.

When they reached a spot where the undergrowth was sparse, they stopped. "I think this is where we went into the woods yesterday," Alex said.

Rocky agreed.

The foursome left the road and headed into the trees.

"The trap was over that way," Rocky said, pointing to his right. "Watch where you step."

They moved cautiously, scanning the ground ahead of them.

"There it is!" Alex said. "It's been reset!"

They looked down at the steel trap.

"There's no ID tag," Mary said.

"Whoever is doing this has been here since we came yesterday," Rocky said. He glanced nervously around, as if expecting the trapper to spring out from behind the bushes and rush toward them.

"I found a clue," Benjie said. He opened his backpack, removed a small plastic bag, and used it to pick up a cigarette butt.

"Anyone walking in the woods might have dropped that," Alex said. "It wasn't necessarily the person who set the trap."

"It was him, and I'm going to save it for evidence. The police can get DNA from a cigarette butt."

"Whether it's evidence or not," Mary said, "it's proof that someone stupid was here."

"Stupid for setting this trap?" Rocky asked.

"That, too, but I meant stupid for smoking in the woods when we're having such dry weather. He could have started a forest fire."

"Smoking wrecks your lungs," Benjie said. "We learned about it in school."

Alex found a thick branch and stuck it in the trap, making the trap snap shut.

Before Benjie put the cigarette butt in his backpack, he removed the cookies and handed two to each person. The chocolate chips had melted slightly, making the cookies taste as if they had just come out of the oven.

After eating their cookies, the kids looked for more traps but found none.

"We'd better start back," Alex said. "Mom and Dad will be home soon."

They made their way out of the woods, then started down the gravel road with Alex and Benjie in the lead.

As they approached a curve in the road, Rocky called, "There's a car coming." He and Mary both moved as far to the side of the road as they could.

Alex heard it, too. It was headed down the hill toward them, and it sounded as if there was a problem with the engine. He took Benjie's hand, and they stepped onto the road's narrow shoulder.

A black pickup truck with slatted wooden sides that went up to the top of the cab careened around the curve.

"He'd better slow down," Alex said. He no sooner got the words out of his mouth than the driver hit the brakes, causing the tires to skid briefly. Gravel flew into the air and clattered back down.

Alex grabbed Benjie's sleeve and pulled him farther off the side of the road, into the brush.

The back end of the truck swung sideways when the brakes grabbed, but then the driver sped up again, and the truck lurched forward. The driver never looked at the four children standing beside the road. As the truck sped downhill past them, the rear of the truck fishtailed again. Dust billowed around the kids, making them cover their noses and mouths to keep from inhaling it.

Alex squinted to avoid getting dust in his eyes, then blinked as something large fell off the back of the truck and landed in the gravel. It was a pig!

"Hey!" Alex shouted, waving his arms over his head and running a few yards down the road behind the truck.

"Stop! You lost your pig!" He saw three other pigs in the back of the truck and feared they would fall out, too.

The truck's brake lights came on for a couple of seconds when Alex yelled, and Alex thought the driver was looking in his rearview mirror, but instead of stopping, the driver hit the gas. The engine roared louder, and the truck sped out of sight.

The pig squealed loudly, tried to stand up, then flopped back down.

3

All of the children rushed toward the pig.
"Those pigs weren't tied to the side or anything," Alex said. "They couldn't keep their balance, and there was nothing to hold them in the truck except that low tailgate."

"The way that guy was driving, it's a wonder all of them didn't fall out," Rocky said.

"Don't touch the pig," Mary warned. "Injured animals can be dangerous."

"We need to get help," Alex said.

The pig made a high-pitched squealing sound.

"Gramma will call the rescue group," Mary said. "Why don't Benjie and I stay here, to be sure no other vehicle comes around the curve and hits the pig. Alex, you and Rocky run back and tell Gramma what happened."

"I want to go, too," Benjie said. "I want to tell about the pig."

"We can run faster without you," Rocky said.

"But . . ."

"I need you to stay here," Mary said, "to help me with the pig."

Alex didn't like leaving Benjie with Mary and the pig, but he knew it was the best plan.

Alex and Rocky ran faster than they ever had before, all the way down the hill, past Hilltop, and into Valley View Estates. They were out of breath when they got to Mrs. Sunburg's house, and had to take turns talking, to tell her what had happened.

"What did the truck look like?" she asked.

They described it.

"Did you get a license-plate number?"

Both boys shook their heads no. "It all happened so fast," Alex said. "I was trying to get the driver's attention. I was looking at him, not at the license plate, plus there was a lot of dust blowing in my face."

"I was watching the pig," Rocky said. "I was afraid it would be killed, falling out like that."

Mrs. Sunburg called the animal rescue group. She repeated the boys' story, gave driving directions, and said, "I'll meet you there." She grabbed her bag of animal first-aid supplies, motioned for Alex and Rocky to follow her, and rushed to her car.

"The rescue group is sending a truck," she said as she drove out of Valley View Estates. "They'll notify the police, too."

By car, it didn't take long to reach the end of the pavement and start up the gravel road. "It isn't far now," Alex said, and Mrs. Sunburg drove slowly.

The pig was still lying in the middle of the road. Mary and Benjie stood in the road about twenty feet from it, one in front of the pig and one on the other side. They waved when they saw the car approaching.

"No other cars came," Benjie said.

"There's a lot of gravel embedded in her skin," Mary said, "and I think one of her legs is hurt. Whenever she tries to stand up, she squeals and flops back down."

"Her name is Piccolo," Benjie said. "Piccolo Pig."

"How do you know that?" Rocky asked.

"Because I named her."

Alex gazed at the enormous pig. Beneath her bristles, the taut skin was as round as a barrel. Clearly this pig had not gone hungry. Thinking of how delicate a piccolo is, he said, "She looks more like a kettle drum than a piccolo."

"She makes a high, shrill noise, like Aunt Jenny's piccolo," Benjie explained and, as if to prove his point, the pig did exactly that.

Mrs. Sunburg slowly approached the pig. The closer she got, the more agitated the pig became. "Easy, girl," Mrs. Sunburg said softly. "We're here to help you."

The pig tried to struggle to her feet, then gave up.

"Pigs are social animals," Mrs. Sunburg said, "but this one is scared and hurt. I don't want to make her injuries worse by having her try to get away from me." She backed away from the pig. "I'll wait for the rescue truck," she said. "Those people are more experienced than I am."

Half an hour later a big white enclosed truck, with graphics of animals painted on the sides, chugged up the hill and came to a stop. Two men hopped out. Both wore caps and navy blue jackets with white lettering that said FOOTHILLS ANIMAL RESCUE.

One man was about the age of Alex's dad. His dark hair was gray at the temples, and his face had a leathery look as if he'd spent years working outdoors. He carried a rope.

The other, younger man had so many rings in his ears that he looked as if he had a spiral notebook on each side of his face. His green hair stood up in short spikes all over his head. "Hey!" he said. "Awesome animal!"

"She's a big one, isn't she?" the older man said.

"Hi, Eric," Mrs. Sunburg said to the older man "Hi, Jacob." She quickly introduced everyone as the two men knelt beside the pig and gently felt for injuries.

"There's no way we can hoist this baby by hand," Eric said. "We'll have to turn the truck around and load her with the lift."

"What can we do to help?" Alex said.

"Stay out of the way, and watch for traffic. Not likely any vehicle will come along, but we need to be alert."

As they talked, the men got the rope tied around the

struggling pig's middle, a feat that took ten minutes and all of their strength. Then Jacob held the end of the rope while Eric turned the truck around.

It wasn't easy to maneuver a U-turn on the narrow gravel road, but Eric managed to do it. Fortunately no other vehicles came along while all this was going on.

Jacob stood beside the pig, his feet braced in the gravel and his hands gripping the rope, trying to control her while the truck backed closer, making a BEEP-BEEP sound that scared the pig even more than she already was.

"Don't be afraid, Piccolo," Benjie said. "He won't hit you."

Alex and Rocky held their hands up, moving them closer together to show Eric how far he was from the pig.

The truck stopped two feet from the pig. Eric got out, rolled the back door up, and pushed a button, which lowered a metal platform down to the gravel. The platform didn't look much bigger than the pig, and Alex wondered how much weight it could hold.

Jacob tossed the end of the rope to Eric, who stood on the platform and pulled while Jacob pushed on the pig's back. She had quit struggling and lay still, as if she had given up and would accept whatever happened. Her eyes still looked fearful, though, and no matter how hard the two men pushed and pulled, the pig didn't budge.

"We'll help," Alex said.

"You kids push," Eric said. "We'll both pull."

Alex, Rocky, Mary, and Benjie lined up along the back side of the pig while Jacob joined Eric on the platform.

"We'll go on the count of three," Eric said. "One. Two. THREE!"

The kids shoved as hard as they could. The two men pulled. The pig squealed her protest as she slowly slid onto the lift. "Now hold her steady," Eric said. "Don't let her roll off."

Eric let go of the rope with one hand long enough to press the lift button; the lift slowly began to rise. Eric and Jacob stayed inside the truck, keeping the rope taut.

Alex knew that he and the others couldn't do anything about it if the heavy pig started to roll off the lift, but he kept his hands firmly on the pig's back as the lift rose. The other kids did the same.

Alex held his breath as the pig rode upward.

"Easy now," Eric said. "Good girl."

When the lift was level with the bed of the truck, it stopped. Eric pushed another button that made the out-side edge of the lift tilt slightly upward. As soon as that happened, the men were able to drag the pig off the lift and onto the floor of the truck. The kids cheered as Jacob rolled the door shut.

"We did it!" Benjie yelled. All the kids high-fived one another while Mrs. Sunburg clapped.

In the midst of the excitement, a police car drove up.

"You the folks who saw a pig fall off a truck?" the police officer asked.

All four kids answered at the same time.

"We were right there, by the curve," Mary said.

"The driver was going way too fast," Alex said. "The back end of the pickup fishtailed when he went around the curve."

"He had three other pigs in the truck, and nothing to keep them from falling out," Rocky said. "This one tumbled right over the tailgate."

"The pig's name is Piccolo," Benjie said, "because she makes a high, squeaky noise."

"Wait, wait," the officer said, holding up his hands. "One at a time." He pointed to Mary. "You first."

Mary told him exactly what had happened, trying to remember every detail.

"The driver didn't see or hear you?" the officer asked.

"I think he saw me," Alex said. "When I yelled at him that he'd lost his pig, he hit the brakes, and I thought he heard me and was going to stop, but he didn't. Instead, he drove away."

Eric spoke next, introducing himself and Jacob. "We're with Foothills Animal Rescue," he said. "We've loaded the hog in our van and we'll take her to a veterinarian. Her injuries don't appear life-threatening, but she's pretty banged up; she'll need treatment."

"You call her a hog, not a pig," Alex said. "What's the difference?"

"When a pig weighs more than one hundred twenty pounds," Eric said, "it's considered a hog. This girl weighs at least twice that much."

"Even though she weighs a lot," Alex said, "I like the word pig better than hog."

"So do I," said Rocky.

"After she's been treated for her wounds," Jacob said, "we'll need a place for her to stay. We're mainly a wildlife rehabilitation group. We sometimes take in domestic animals, but our shelter isn't really equipped for farm animals. That's one big porker."

"We'll take her," Benjie said.

"Where are we going to keep a pig?" Alex asked.

"At Mrs. Sunburg's house. She's a foster parent for the animals."

"Pigs make wonderful pets," Mrs. Sunburg said, "but I would need to have a pen built. A pig that size needs plenty of space."

"We could build a pen for you," Alex said.

"My dad will help," Benjie said.

"We'll all help." Rocky looked hopefully at Mrs. Sunburg.

"Please, Gramma?" Mary said. "I'll take care of her. I'll muck out the pen and feed her."

"The vet could probably keep the pig overnight," Eric said. "Can you have a pen ready by tomorrow?"

"Yes!" the kids replied.

"A pen may not be necessary," the police officer said. "There are only a few houses in this area; it shouldn't be too hard to find out who owns this animal."

"Surely you don't plan to give the pig back to that truck driver," Mrs. Sunburg said. "If you find him, it seems to me he should be ticketed for having an unsafe load."

"She's right," Eric said. "It isn't legal to endanger an animal while transporting it."

"He was speeding," Mary said. "We can all testify to that."

"He didn't stop at the scene of an accident," Alex said. "That's a crime, too."

The police officer looked from one to the next.

"I agree that you need to find that truck driver," Jacob said, "but not to return the hog. Find Hogman so you can file charges."

"For people who just happened to see a pig fall off a truck, you all seem to know a lot about the law."

"I'm a licensed humane officer," Eric said.

"I'm a trained animal rescue worker," Mrs. Sunburg said.

"I'm a spy," Benjie said.

The officer nodded. Then he wrote down each of their names, addresses, and telephone numbers. "Since the driver left the scene," he said, "I'm giving temporary custody of the hog to Foothills Animal Rescue."

"As long as you're here," Alex said, "do you want to see the illegal leghold trap that someone has set in the woods? It's not far."

"That's a matter for the game warden," the officer said. He got back in his car.

They watched the patrol car turn around, then drive away.

"I don't think finding the pig's owner is going to be a high-priority item with the police," Alex said.

"You're right," Eric said. "This county has unsolved murders and robberies, to say nothing of the large number of meth labs. The cops don't have time to look for that truck driver."

"He broke the law," Benjie said. "He shouldn't get away with it."

"We saved the pig," Mary said, "and that's what matters."

"If the owner isn't found, we get to keep the pig," Alex said.

"Let's go," Eric said to Jacob. "This little piggy needs to get to the vet."

"Call us when you know how she is," Mrs. Sunburg said.

"We'll start building the pen," Alex said.

"Good luck, Piccolo," Benjie called as the truck drove off. "I hope your leg is okay."

4

Benjie dashed into the house first, shouting, "We rescued a pig! Her name is Piccolo, and we're keeping her!"

"A *pig!*" Pete said. *"Oh, no. We are not adopting any pig. Forget it. I was a good sport when you brought a kitten into the house, but there's no way I'm sharing my food bowl and my litter box with a pig!" He flattened his ears, made the fur stand up on his back, and growled.*

"Where on earth did you find a pig?" Mrs. Kendrill asked.

Alex, Rocky, Mary, and Mrs. Sunburg explained what had happened.

"A pig is even better than a rhinoceros," Benjie said.

"I checked the zoning regulations about animals before I bought my place," Mrs. Sunburg said. "It would be all right to keep a pig on my property, providing the neighbors don't object."

"We're the neighbors," Alex said. "We won't object."

"*I object!*" *Pete said.* "*Do you know how much kitty num-num a pig would eat?*"

"I've always thought it would be fun to have a pet pig," Mary said. "They're very intelligent animals."

"*Not as intelligent as cats,*" *Pete said.*

"They're even smarter than dogs," Mary said.

"*Well, that doesn't take much,*" *Pete said.*

"Except for humans and the great apes," Mrs. Sunburg said, "pigs are the most intelligent animals there are."

Pete growled. "*I beg to differ with you. How many pigs do you know who can read? How many pigs have written a book? How many pigs can tell you what a CAT scan is?*"

"Alex, would you please feed Pete?" Mrs. Kendrill said.

"He doesn't need food," Alex said. "I think he's just excited."

"Then shut him in the bathroom while we talk," she said. "He makes such a racket, I can hardly think."

"*Racket? You call my valued opinion a racket? I'm telling you, not all animals are created equal. Adopting a pig would be a catastrophe!*"

Alex started toward Pete.

"*Watch this,*" *Pete said. He ran to the base of the entertainment center, crouched, moved his hind feet up and down a couple of times, then propelled himself upward. Ever since he had read the definition of "catapult" in Alex's diction-*

ary—"a device for launching an airplane at flying speed; to throw or launch as if by a catapult"—he had been doing this trick.

He landed with a thud on top of the entertainment center. "Did you see me?" he called. "I'm a catapulting cat! How many pigs can do that?"

"Mercy," Mrs. Kendrill said. "There he goes again."

"I love it when he does that," Mary said.

"That's quite a leap for a cat," Mrs. Sunburg said, "especially one his size."

"I'm solid muscle," Pete replied. He wished the humans wouldn't keep mentioning his size. In Pete's opinion, they put way too much emphasis on being slender—especially that uninformed veterinarian who kept suggesting diet cat food.

Lizzy ran to the base of the entertainment center and looked up at Pete, but she didn't try to jump.

"Will you help us build a pigpen?" Alex asked his dad. "I'll pay for part of the lumber. I have eighteen dollars saved."

"We need to hear the vet's report before we do that," Mr. Kendrill said. "The pig could have serious injuries. They might not be able to save her."

"Piccolo can't die," Benjie said, his eyes puddling with tears. "She's the best pig in the world."

"Her wounds looked treatable," Mrs. Sunburg said, "but there's always the possibility of internal injuries."

"I suppose it won't hurt to draw up some plans for a pen," Mr. Kendrill said. "We can figure out where it would go and what materials we would need."

"Pigs smell bad," Pete said. "They don't bathe themselves the way cats do. Don't expect me to wash her ears for her."

"Let's go take a look at my yard," Mrs. Sunburg suggested, "to see where a pigpen might go." She opened the door, and everyone trooped out behind her.

Pete quickly put his front paws on the entertainment center and let them slide down while he kept his balance with his back legs. Catapulting up was a lot faster and more fun than getting down again. Although Pete hurried, he didn't make it to the floor in time to follow his family outside.

Annoyed with them for not waiting for him, he went up to Alex's room. Good. Alex had left the dictionary on his desk. It was much easier to look up words if Pete didn't have to pull the thick book from the bookcase before he could read it. Pete hopped on the desk, turned the pages until he came to the c-a-t section, and began to read.

Even though he had read this section of the dictionary many times before, he read slowly and carefully. In Pete's experience, words had a way of calling attention to themselves at the very moment when they would be most useful. That's what had happened the day he learned "catapult." Right when he needed a way to get his family's attention, there was the perfect word, and Pete had been catapulting ever since.

This time, his eyes stopped on the word "caterwaul." He read the definition: "to make a harsh cry." Pete took a deep breath and let out a loud, shrill screech. Lizzy rushed into the room, her yellow eyes wide and wondering.

"I'm caterwauling," Pete explained, and he screeched again. The fur on Lizzy's tail puffed up, and she ran back downstairs.

Pete's voice echoed in Alex's room, as if more than one cat had howled. Very satisfying, Pete thought, and certain to be noticed. Perhaps after he perfected his caterwauling, he would try caterwauling and catapulting at the same time. That ought to be exciting enough to make his people forget about adopting a silly pig.

Satisfied with his new skill, Pete returned to the kitchen. After emptying his bowl of crunchies, he curled up under the table, in the spot where the afternoon sun came through the window. Soon Lizzy lay down beside him. Pete washed her ears for her, licking vigorously until they were clean, while Lizzy purred and kneaded her toenails in and out of the carpet.

That was the kitten's best trait: she let him wash her ears. He had often tried to wash the humans' ears, but they didn't understand that Pete was grooming them and making them more attractive.

Once, Pete had sneaked into bed with Alex's parents while they were asleep, and had started licking Mrs.

Kendrill's ear. Talk about caterwauling! Mrs. Kendrill had made the loudest, most harsh noise Pete had ever heard, to say nothing of the fact that she had rudely shoved him off the bed without so much as an apology.

Pete licked Lizzy's ears until he grew sleepy, then stretched full-length in the sun, and closed his eyes for a catnap.

Half an hour later, the Kendrills returned. Alex and his dad sat at the table with graph paper, pencils, and a ruler. They drew up plans for a pigpen and made a list of the supplies needed to build it.

"I'm going to my spy headquarters," Benjie said. "Let me know if you hear anything about Piccolo." He picked up his binoculars and his backpack, then opened the cookie jar.

Mrs. Kendrill said, "No more cookies, Benjie. You've had enough."

"Just one?" Benjie said. "I'm going to watch for flying green panthers and falling pigs and bad guys who trap animals. I might even see a singing camel that's escaped from a zoo. I'll get hungry!"

"You can take an apple," Mrs. Kendrill said. As the door closed behind Benjie, she added, "If that boy can channel his imagination into writing books or movies, he'll be famous when he grows up."

Alex and his dad had just finished making their list when

the phone rang. "Gramma heard from the vet," Mary told Alex. "The pig's going to be fine. If we can have the pen ready, Eric and Jacob will deliver her at noon tomorrow."

Alex turned to his dad. "The pig's okay. Can we have the pen done by noon tomorrow?"

"I don't see why not, especially if we have help."

"We'll be ready," Alex told Mary.

"You're making a big mistake," Pete said. "Pigs can't even purr, and as for sitting on your lap, forget it."

"Mary says the pig needs a scratching post," Alex said as he replaced the phone.

"Scratching posts are for cats," Pete said. He used his often, to sharpen his front claws. He would prefer to use the Kendrills' sofa, but the humans didn't like it when he did that, so he settled for the carpet-covered post in the corner, attacking it with his claws extended, tearing bits of the carpet loose. He tried to imagine a pig doing that, but he couldn't. Pigs have no claws, only those clunky hooves. Why would a pig need a scratching post?

Alex was apparently thinking the same thing because he said, "The pig must use a post to rub against, to groom herself."

"No wonder pigs smell," Pete said, "if their idea of grooming is to rub against a post. You'd stink, too, if all you did was rub against the shower door instead of turning on the water."

"I'll call Rocky and see if he and his dad can help build the pen tomorrow morning," Alex said.

"We can go to the lumber store now," Mr. Kendrill said, "and get what we need. Tell them we'll meet tomorrow at eight."

While Alex was talking to Rocky, Benjie dashed in. "I saw Hogman!" he shouted.

"Who?" Mr. Kendrill asked.

"I saw the man in the truck that Piccolo was in when she fell off. He went up the main road toward Hilltop, and he was driving slow this time. He's probably looking for Piccolo!"

"Were the other pigs still in the back of the truck?" Alex asked.

"Nope. It was empty, but I know it was the same truck; it had those wooden slats on the sides and it was dirty and the engine made a lot of noise."

"Did the man see you?"

Benjie shook his head no. "I was hiding in my spy bush and I stayed really still."

"Did you get a license-plate number?" Mr. Kendrill asked.

"No."

That surprised Alex, because Benjie took his spy games seriously. Alex would have expected him to either memorize the number or write it down.

"Why would I want his number?" Benjie asked. "I don't want to talk to that man. I don't want him to find Piccolo."

"Now, Benjie," Mrs. Kendrill said. "If the pig belongs to the man in the truck, and if the man wants her back, we may have to let him take her."

"The police gave custody of the pig to the rescue group," Alex said. He saw no need to mention that it was temporary custody.

"Maybe he won't find her," Benjie said, his lip quivering as if he were about to burst into tears.

Mrs. Kendrill sighed, but said no more.

"He might not have been looking for Piccolo," Alex told Benjie. "Maybe he lives up the hill, and he was going home."

At eight the next morning, Pete stayed close to the kitchen door, watching for a chance to run out and join the neighborhood group that planned to build the pigpen. Alex carried two hammers, a box of nails, and a yardstick, but even with his hands full, he stuck his foot in Pete's path while he went out the door, keeping the cat inside.

Mr. and Mrs. Kendrill shooed him away as they left, too. Pete knew his best chance to escape was to wait for Benjie, who had lingered to fill his pockets with cookies.

As Benjie hurried to the door, Pete followed him, and when Benjie went out, Pete dashed out, too. Benjie pulled the door shut, never noticing Pete, who loped across the yard toward Mrs. Sunburg's property.

Pete watched from under a bush as Mr. Kendrill supervised construction. Pete's whiskers twitched at the smell of the cedar fence posts.

The people dug postholes six feet apart, pounded the wooden posts into the holes, then dumped wet concrete, which they had mixed in a wheelbarrow, into the holes. Rocky held a level against the side of each post, to be sure it was straight.

"We really should let that concrete set before we put the fencing on," Mr. Kendrill said, "but there isn't time to wait. Try not to wiggle the posts as you work."

Alex and Rocky held the posts in place while the adults stretched sturdy wire fencing between each post. Mary stapled the fencing on with heavy metal staples.

A hinged gate with a latch went on the side of the pen facing Mary's house. When the pen was finished, the group built a three-sided shed, with a roof, in one corner of the pen, where Piccolo would have shelter from rain and sun. Last they put in one free-standing post, for the pig to rub against.

It wouldn't be as good as living inside with a family, Pete thought, but it was a fine-looking animal house. If animals rated their lodging the way people rate hotel rooms, Pete would give the pigpen four stars.

Mary filled a metal pail with water and put it in one corner of the pen. Rocky set a large tin trough beside it, then dumped in a bucket of table scraps that he had collected from around the neighborhood.

Pete's mouth dropped open in astonishment as he saw toast crusts, leftover ham-and-cheese omelet, half a peanut-butter sandwich, and some green-bean casserole drop into the trough. That was the biggest dinner bowl he'd ever seen! He wondered how many cans of kitty num-num it would hold. Fifty? Sixty? Maybe even one hundred! He upped the pigpen's rating to five stars. Pete would be willing to sleep in that shed himself if it meant a bowl of food that big.

At eleven, the crew took a break. Mrs. Sunburg passed around a plate of blueberry muffins while Rocky's mom offered cans of apple juice and bottled water.

"Do we need old blankets or towels for Piccolo to sleep on?" Benjie asked.

"Eric said he'd bring hay for bedding," Mrs. Sunburg said.

Promptly at noon the rescue truck drove in. By then the pen was finished. The truck backed up to it, positioning the lift in front of the pen's gate.

"Hey!" Eric said as he jumped out of the truck. "That's a mighty impressive pigpen!"

"For an awesome pig," said Jacob, who got out of the passenger side.

"How's Piccolo?" Benjie asked.

"Her leg is still sore," Eric said, "and it will take a while for the cuts and scrapes to heal, but she was full of energy this morning. The vet gave her a mild tranquilizer before we loaded her on the truck, so she's sleepy right now and will probably snooze away the afternoon."

"Let's move her before the tranquilizer wears off," said Jacob.

Alex unlatched the gate and swung it open while Eric and Jacob rolled up the truck's door. They shoved the pig onto the lift, then Eric pushed the button, and the lift slowly lowered. When it reached the ground, Eric pushed the control again, causing the side of the lift next to the truck to raise slightly, letting the pig roll gently into the pen.

Next the men tossed several bales of hay from the truck into the pen. Alex, Rocky, Mary, and Benjie spread hay on the ground under the roofed area of the pen.

When they finished, Mary said, "There you go, Piccolo. Your bed is ready."

Piccolo didn't move. Benjie stood beside her, petting her. When Piccolo didn't respond, the kids left the pen. Alex closed the gate, and Rocky snapped a padlock on it.

Eric said, "I did some checking about that trap you found. A couple of months ago a report was filed by a couple in Hilltop whose German shepherd got caught in a leghold trap in that same area. They found their dog, cut the trap off with a hacksaw, and got the dog to a vet in time to save it. The trap had no tag, and the trapper was never caught."

"Isn't there something we can do to stop him?" Alex asked.

"It's a hard law to enforce," Eric said. "We do our best, but there aren't nearly enough game wardens or humane officers to cover a county this size. Now that I know about the problem, I'll drive up that road whenever I'm in this area."

"The chance of actually catching the trapper in the act of trapping is practically nil," Jacob said, "but sometimes if people see the rescue truck in the area, that alone makes them hesitate about breaking an animal-related law."

"We'll take a drive up there right now," Eric said, "before we head back to town."

Jacob and Eric shook hands all around before they drove off in the rescue truck.

Benjie stood beside the pen, gazing at the sleeping pig. "Isn't she beautiful?" he said.

Pete stared at the pig's round belly. Talk about corpulent! She resembled the big balloons that Pete saw in the Thanksgiving Day Parade each year. If Doctor Uninformed thought Pete, who was actually the perfect size, needed diet cat food, he would surely say this animal was a serious candidate for diet pig food. Instead the humans were feeding her leftover omelets and toast.

After everyone had admired the pig and the new pen for a few minutes, Mr. Kendrill said, "I'm heading home. I have work to do."

"Thanks for helping us, everybody," Alex said.

"It was good to have a neighborhood project," Rocky's mom said. "We don't get together often enough."

The adults left, but the kids stayed. They wanted to watch the pig awhile, even if all she did was sleep.

Pete stayed, too, although it was time for his lunch and his afternoon nap in the sunny spot under the table. He was too curious about the pig to leave her. He wanted to see what would happen when she woke up, and he wondered if she might be able to understand Cat.

5

Alex was shocked to see Piccolo on the five o'clock news. He was sitting on the floor combing Pete while Benjie sat beside him, building a miniature pig-pen out of LEGOS. Their mom clicked on the TV news while she prepared dinner.

Pete didn't like to be combed, but he tolerated it because Alex wanted to do it. Alex thought combing prevented Pete from getting hair balls, which the people mistakenly believed were undesirable. The humans didn't understand how satisfying it was to retch and gag and finally expel a big wad of undigested cat fur onto the carpet.

It was especially gratifying to urp up a hair ball in the middle of the night. The humans always leaped from their beds and came running in their pajamas and their bare feet, hoping to reach him before the hair ball eruption so they could remove him from the carpet and put him on the bathroom's tile floor.

Of course, they never arrived in time, but their hasty actions added a good bit of interest to an otherwise dull night. It had been particularly exciting the night that Mr. Kendrill failed to see the freshly deposited hair ball until he stepped in it, although Pete saw no reason for anyone to shout over what was clearly an unintentional accident. Humans tend to be cranky when they're awakened abruptly.

A cat's stomach is a marvelous creation of Nature, Pete thought, looking fondly at his own substantial belly. It comes equipped with the perfect mechanism to rid the body of any fur that gets swallowed as a result of keeping oneself clean.

The humans thought they had a better plan. Every time Pete coughed up a hair ball, Mrs. Kendrill reminded Alex that he needed to comb Pete every day.

Pete allowed Alex to run the cat comb through his fur, but he knew that if he continued to groom himself and Lizzy, he could easily ingest enough fur to make another hair ball before long.

Since having to clean the carpet distressed the Kendrills, Pete decided that the next time he urped up a hair ball he would do it in the kitchen, while they were cooking dinner. That would help them understand how efficient cats are, and how willing to compromise.

Alex continued to run the comb down Pete's back as the news announcer talked about trouble in the Middle East and a political scandal in Washington, D.C., and the arrest of a man suspected of burglarizing three convenience stores. Alex tuned out until he heard the announcer say, "We have an unusual animal rescue to tell you about tonight. Stay tuned for details of the pig who escaped slaughter by jumping off a truck."

Alex grabbed the phone and dialed Rocky's number. "Turn on channel four," he said. Before Rocky could reply, Alex hung up and called Mary, telling her the same thing.

When the commercials ended, the TV screen showed Piccolo being examined by a veterinarian. The announcer told how some children had seen the pig fall off the truck, how the driver failed to stop, and how Foothills Animal Rescue had taken the pig to the veterinarian.

"The pig weighs two hundred fifty pounds," the vet said, "so she's about eight months old. That's when pigs are usually slaughtered. If she had not fallen off the truck, she'd probably be pork chops by now."

"The pig was treated for her wounds and released to the rescue group," the announcer said. "They have found a permanent home for her in the rural community of Valley View Estates, not far from where she jumped to freedom."

The weatherman came on next, but Mrs. Kendrill turned the TV off. "I wonder who notified the TV station," she said.

"Why did they have to say where Piccolo is?" Alex said.

"If Hogman knows she's in our neighborhood, he might come looking for her."

Pete felt chilled by the casual way the human had talked about pork chops. Pete didn't want to share his family's love and attention with the pig, but he didn't want her made into pork chops and eaten for dinner, either. The pig was an animal, just as Pete was an animal. He didn't think the humans ever ate cat chops, but even so, such talk made him uneasy.

As soon as they finished dinner, Alex and Benjie went over to Mary's house to check on Piccolo. Because they were talking about the TV broadcast, Alex forgot to watch for Pete, who slithered out and followed them.

Mary was in the pen, sitting beside the pig, who was still dozing. "Right after that news broadcast," she said, "Eric called to ask if we had contacted the TV station. Gramma told him no and said she thought he might have done it. He hadn't, so Gramma called the TV station and asked how they found out about the pig."

"Would they tell her?" Alex asked. "I think their sources are confidential."

"They said one of their reporters regularly monitors the police radio and when she heard the call about the pig, she thought it would make a good human-interest story. She got a cameraman, looked up which veterinarian was closest to where the pig was found, and went there. By the time she arrived, Eric and Jacob had left on another rescue call, but the reporter interviewed the veterinarian and filmed her treating Piccolo."

"I wish the vet hadn't said the name of our housing development," Alex said.

"Me, too."

"Maybe Hogman won't see the news broadcast," Alex said.

"Maybe," Mary agreed, "although the stations usually broadcast stories like that several times. You can watch the news on Sunday morning and see exactly the same thing you saw Saturday night."

Alex knew she was right. He also knew that if the man learned where Piccolo was, it could mean problems ahead.

Pete was the first to hear the rumbling engine of the old pickup truck as it drove slowly down the street.

Alex heard it next.

"Listen," Alex said, holding up one finger to shush the other kids. "That sounds like the truck Piccolo fell out of."

"Hogman's looking for Piccolo," Benjie whispered. "I knew it! He's driving all around trying to find her."

"He doesn't know she's here," Mary said. "If he did, he'd come down the driveway."

Alex went to the corner of Mrs. Sunburg's house and peered around it, looking toward the street.

"Don't let him see you," Mary said. "He might recognize you from yesterday, when you yelled at him to stop."

Alex was glad they had built the pen in a part of the yard that didn't show from the street. All of the lots in Valley View Estates were at least two acres, with many trees. He saw Hogman's truck go toward the cul-de-sac at the end of the street, and then a few minutes later, it cruised back the way it had come.

The kids were silent, listening until the rattle of the truck faded away.

"He must have seen that news story," Rocky said.

"Maybe not," Mary said. "Our houses aren't far from where Piccolo fell off the truck. Hogman might be driving aimlessly around, hoping to see a lost pig. He'll probably quit looking for her in a day or two. He'll think she got hurt when she fell, and went into the woods and died."

Alex hoped Mary was right. Although he'd never met the driver of that truck, he didn't like the man and didn't want a confrontation with him, no matter who had official custody of Piccolo.

By morning, the pig's tranquilizer had worn off. Alex hurried over right after breakfast and found Mary already in the pen. Rocky arrived a few minutes later.

"She likes to be scratched behind her ears," Mary said. "She seems happy and friendly today."

"She knows we saved her," Alex said.

Pete, who had climbed out of Alex's bedroom window and

*then down the maple tree, sat in his hiding place under the
bush and watched as Alex entered the pigpen and began petting the pig.*

"She's really clean," Mary said. "She uses that far corner of the pen for her bathroom, and she goes there every
time."

"Good Piccolo," said Rocky. "What a smart pig."

*Big whoop-de-do, thought Pete. Cats do the same thing,
and nobody ever makes a big fuss over us. Even Lizzy, who
can't read, write, or understand humans, knows enough to
use the litter pan.*

"After her wounds heal, maybe we can give her a bath,"
Alex said. "She may be smart, but she smells like a full
garbage can."

Ha! thought Pete. Finally someone speaks the truth.

"I read about pigs on the Internet last night," Rocky
said. "They're supposed to smell the way they do because
pigs leave many smells on everything they pass. It's their
way of showing who they are."

"You're saying even if we bathe her, she'll still smell?"
Mary asked.

"That's right."

*Pete decided to do some research of his own when he had
a chance. Maybe he could find a reason why his family
should not keep a pig.*

"There's a lot of information about pigs," Rocky said.

"When I have time, I'm going to find out when piggy banks were invented and what it means when someone goes hog wild."

"What about living high on the hog?" Mary asked. "What is a pig in a poke?"

Alex began rubbing the pig's head, behind her ears. Piccolo responded by grunting. Alex rubbed the pig's neck. Piccolo leaned against him, with her eyes closed.

Piccolo sat down. Alex kept rubbing. The pig lowered her front legs, then suddenly collapsed, falling over on her side with an OOOMPH! sound.

Pete watched in astonishment as the pig rolled on her back with her feet in the air.

"She wants a belly rub!" Alex said, clearly delighted, and he began rubbing the pig's stomach with the flat of his hand. Mary and Rocky joined in.

"Piccolo's in hog heaven," Mary said, and all the kids laughed.

Pete glared at them from under the bush. It wasn't funny. Alex was giving that pig a kitty massage! How could he be so disloyal? Kitty massages were Pete's treat, something Alex had always done only for him. Even Lizzy didn't get kitty massages. Now Alex, Rocky, and Mary all bent over the pig, rubbing and scratching on her fat pink stomach as if the pig were queen of the universe and they were her privileged servants.

Pete's tail whipped furiously back and forth, sending a swirl of dust into the air.

Suddenly the pig raised her head, struggled to a sitting position, and then stood up, her big ears pricked forward. She gave a sharp, abrupt grunt that sounded almost like a sneeze.

A second later, Pete heard that engine sound again—the rattling noise that had upset Alex when he heard it the day before.

The pig grunted again, then began clicking her teeth. Pete looked at the pig with new respect. Cats have astute hearing, but the pig had heard that engine even before Pete had. The sharp grunt and the clicking teeth must be her alarm call, warning the people that the truck was coming.

The people paid no attention. Obviously they did not understand Pig any better than they understood Cat.

The engine noise grew louder. Alex turned toward it and saw his little brother, tears streaming down his cheeks, running down the driveway toward the Kendrills' house. The truck that the pig had jumped from rolled along right behind Benjie.

"Oh, oh," Alex said. "This looks like trouble."

The three kids quickly left the pigpen. Mary closed the padlock, clicking it shut. As they headed into Alex's yard, toward Benjie, the truck stopped and the driver got out, leaving the door open. He wore stained jeans and muddy boots. His greasy hair grazed the collar of his dirty blue shirt.

Hogman. Alex thought the name Jacob had given the truck's driver made him sound greedy and in need of a bath. It seemed to fit.

"He saw me on the corner when I was playing spy," Benjie cried. "He asked me where I live, but I didn't tell him. I ran for home, but he followed me."

"I'm not gonna hurt you, kid," the man said. "I only wanted to ask if you knew where my pig was, but that question's been answered." He pointed at Mary's backyard, in the direction of the pen. His hand looked as if it had not touched soap and water for weeks. "There she is, right there."

"Go get Dad," Alex told Benjie.

Benjie hurried toward the kitchen door.

6

"You must be the kids who found my pig on the road," the man said.

Alex, Rocky, and Mary looked at him, but nobody spoke.

"What's the matter?" the man said. "The cat got your tongues?"

Pete, who was listening from under his bush, growled softly. What a horrid thing to say! As if a cat would take the tongue out of a child, or anyone else. Where do the humans come up with such nonsense? To say, "The cat got your tongue," was even worse than calling a thief a "cat burglar."

"That pig belongs to me," the man continued. "I'll drive my truck over to the pen, then you all can help me get her loaded."

"You'll have to talk to my gramma first," Mary said.

"Don't need to talk to anybody. Only need to load up my pig."

"Gramma has the key to the pigpen," Mary said. "The gate's locked."

"That your gramma's house?" The dirty hand pointed again.

Mary nodded.

"Go get her while I move my truck," the man said. He got in the vehicle, turned it around, and drove off. Seconds later, he had driven down Mary's driveway and was backing up to the pigpen. Again, he left the truck door open when he got out.

Alex and Rocky had cut across the yard and were already standing in front of the pen. Mary had gone inside.

"I ain't got all day," the man said. "You sure you kids don't have a key to that gate?"

"I don't have one," Alex said.

"Neither do I," said Rocky.

They knew Mary had the key, but they weren't going to mention that.

Mrs. Sunburg and Mary came out of the house together. "What's going on here?" Mrs. Sunburg asked.

"That's my pig," the man said. "I came to get her. I have a rope and a ramp. I'll put her on my truck as soon as y'all open the pen."

"Can you prove this pig belongs to you?" Alex asked.

"Prove? I don't need to prove anything. It's my pig! I

was driving down the road when she fell off my truck, and when I went back to get her, she was gone. Stole! My brother saw on the TV news that some kids found her and took her to Valley View Estates. This is Valley View Estates, ain't it?"

"It is," Mrs. Sunburg said.

"Well, then, that proves the pig's mine. Now if you'll kindly open that lock, I'll take my property and leave."

"The fact that this is Valley View Estates doesn't prove who owns the pig," Mary said.

The man glared at her.

"I've called the animal rescue group that delivered Piccolo here," Mrs. Sunburg said. "They have custody of this pig, and they entrusted her to me. I can't let her go."

"Then I'll have to take her without your permission because she belongs to me."

Mrs. Sunburg folded her arms across her chest. "If you touch that pig, I'll call the police."

"Police!" He spit out the word as if it tasted bitter. "Why would you call the cops?"

"Because you broke the law by not keeping the pig safe in your truck," Alex said.

"You also left the scene of an accident," Rocky said.

"I wasn't in any accident. It's not my fault if the stupid pig jumped off the truck."

"The police gave custody of this pig to the Foothills

Animal Rescue," Mrs. Sunburg said. "You'll need to discuss the matter with them or with the police."

"I ain't talking to no cops," the man said.

While the people argued, Pete crept out from under his bush and slowly approached the open door of the truck. The distinct odor of a fried-egg-and-cheese sandwich wafted out of the cab, making Pete curious to see what Hogman might have on the seat. Had he just come from Mad Dogs Café or McDonald's? Was there a bite or two of sandwich left in the wrapper, lying on the seat?

Pete stood on his hind legs and stretched up to look inside the truck. He froze, forgetting all about a possible sandwich. What he saw in the truck was a far worse horror than anything he had ever seen or could have imagined. The fur rose along the ridge of Pete's spine, and his tail bushed out to twice its normal size.

"Hey! Get away from my truck, cat!"

Pete jumped at the sudden shout, then raced away from the truck as fast as he could run. Behind him, he heard the slam of the truck's door. Pete climbed the nearest tree, clung to a low branch, then peered down through the leaves. Although he knew he was safe, the memory of what he'd seen made his heart pound and kept every nerve on edge.

The man sat in the truck now, talking through the open window. "I'll be back," he said, "and I'll have someone with me, to help load MY pig. The gate on that pen had better be unlocked when I get here because I'll have my wire cutters in my pocket, and I'll use them if I need to."

He started the engine, turned around on Mrs. Sunburg's grass, and drove off.

Mr. Kendrill, his hair still damp, rushed across the yard beside Benjie. He buttoned his shirt as he approached. "I was in the shower," he said. "I came as fast as I could. What happened?"

As the others explained, Benjie started to cry again. "That meanie man's going to take Piccolo," he sobbed.

Alex wanted to console his brother, but he was afraid Benjie might be right.

Pete dug his toenails into the tree branch, shaken by what he had seen. A large box on the floor of the truck overflowed with animal skins! Pete had seen dead animals before, usually along the side of a busy road, but he had never seen pelts, and he shuddered as he thought how the pelts must have been obtained.

"Maybe Eric and Jacob can come," Mary suggested. "If they get here before the man returns, they'd know how to handle this."

"They can't come," Mrs. Sunburg said. "When I called to tell them he was here, they were on their way to investigate a cruelty case and said they'd probably be there all morning. That's why I threatened to call the police. I don't really want to do that, though. The police are too busy to deal with a situation like this where nobody's in danger."

"Piccolo's in danger!" Benjie said. "If that meanie Hogman takes her away, she'll be made into pork chops. The man on TV said so."

"Maybe that's who we should call," Alex said. "The TV station that ran the story on Piccolo might be interested in doing a follow-up."

"That's a great idea," Mr. Kendrill said. "There's always a need for human-interest stories about animals."

"The man might not be in such a hurry to use his wire cutters on our pen if there's a news camera here, recording everything," Mrs. Sunburg said.

"Let's go call right now," Mary said.

While the people went inside Mary's house, Pete stretched his front paws down the tree trunk and used his back feet to keep himself from sliding down too fast. When he was five feet from the ground, he shoved off with his hind feet and leaped to the ground. Then he ran for home and waited on the back steps of his house for Alex to return.

When Alex, Benjie, and Mr. Kendrill approached, Pete said, "I looked in Hogman's truck and it's full of animal pelts. I think he's the one who's setting traps! Either that, or he's hunting out of season. You need to call the Department of Fish and Wildlife and have them send someone here. When Hogman returns, I can show them the evidence."

"Stop complaining, Pete," Alex said. "If you wouldn't sneak out, you wouldn't have to wait to be let back in."

"*I'm not asking to be let in,*" *Pete said.* "*I'm telling you I found proof of a catastrophic crime!*"

"Make sure he has cat food," Mr. Kendrill said as he held the door for Pete.

"*Forget the cat food,*" *Pete said.* "*If we're going to eat, let's have fried-egg-and-cheese sandwiches. I had my heart set on one of those; that's what I smelled when I looked in Hogman's truck.*"

Alex poured dry cat food into Pete's bowl while Pete rubbed against his ankles. "There you go, Pete," he said as he set the bowl on the floor.

"*That is not a fried-egg-and-cheese sandwich,*" *Pete said.* "*It isn't even kitty num-num.*" *Kitty num-num came in small cans, labeled "Ocean Whitefish and Tuna." He usually got kitty num-num only at night because Alex used it as a bribe to make sure Pete came home before dark, but once in a while he got it as a reward.*

He had hoped such important news as the box of pelts would merit a reward, but, as usual, the humans were not clever enough to figure out what Pete was telling them. The schools really should offer Cat as a second language.

He sighed, settled himself in front of his bowl, and began to eat. While he would have preferred a fried-egg-and-cheese sandwich or some kitty num-num, Pete appreciated the sat-

isfying "crunch" sound that dry cat food made when he bit it. Pete chewed, pretending the cat food was mouse bones.

"What will we do if the man returns before the TV reporter gets here?" Benjie asked.

"We'll stall him," Alex said.

"I'm going to sit by Piccolo's pen and guard her," Benjie said.

"I'll be there in a few minutes," Alex said, "as soon as I get something to eat."

Benjie left, letting the door bang behind him.

"I still can't believe your good luck in getting to talk to that reporter," Mr. Kendrill told Alex. "I thought you'd get voice mail and have to leave a message."

"I did get voice mail," Alex said, "but the message gave a number to use if the call was about a breaking news story. When I called that number, the reporter answered. Her name is Jenna."

Pete stopped eating so he could hear the conversation. He had planned to take a nap now, but he would need to stay alert so that he could sneak out the door in time to see the reporter. If Hogman returned, Pete would go in the truck again and then holler at the people. He would caterwaul so they'd come and find the box of animal pelts, and they'd arrest Hogman for illegally trapping animals. Pete would be a hero! He'd be the lead story on the five o'clock news! That would show the people which animal is most intelligent.

Of course, he'd have to be careful not to let Hogman see him go in the truck. Anyone who killed animals and skinned them should be avoided, especially by a curious cat.

The dark brown pelts in Hogman's box were beautiful, but not as lovely as Pete's soft white-and-brown fur. He didn't think the humans ever wore coats made of cat fur, but he wasn't positive about that. If they wore mink and beaver and rabbit fur, why not cat?

7

I want to wait in the pen with Piccolo," Benjie said. "I'm going to comb her." He took his own comb out of his back pocket and showed it to Alex.

"You should wait a while before you go in the pen," Alex said. "The gate needs to stay locked in case Hogman returns."

"Then I'll go to the corner and wait in my spy station," Benjie said. "When the TV people come, I can show them where Piccolo is."

Alex watched his brother run down the driveway. He knew Benjie was too antsy to stay in one place very long, and Alex didn't blame him. He felt uneasy himself, and he could tell that Rocky and Mary were anxious, too.

Relax, Alex told himself. Dad's home, and Mrs. Sunburg is home, and the reporter is on her way. If the man got obnoxious, the adults would handle him, or they'd call the police.

"I've gotten really fond of Piccolo," Mary said, "even though she's only been here one day. She's such a friendly pig. It's almost as if she knows we rescued her."

Pete, who had leaped over Alex's foot when Alex tried to keep him inside, shook his head in disbelief. Well, of course she knows, he thought. The pig might not be as smart as a cat, but she wasn't stupid. Humans didn't give animals enough credit.

"Maybe Hogman won't be put off by publicity," Alex said. "If he thinks he has a right to take the pig, maybe he won't care who sees him do it."

"He might want to be on television," Rocky said. "Have you noticed how people react when they see someone with a big video camera? They wave and jump up and down and hold signs; they act ridiculous, trying to call attention to themselves so they'll be on TV."

It was true, Alex thought. Maybe his idea of calling the reporter hadn't been so great, after all.

"Gramma called the police department's nonemergency line and told them the situation," Mary said. "If that man comes back for Piccolo, we're not supposed to try to stop him."

"What?" Alex said. "We're supposed to let him take the pig?"

"We're supposed to call 911, and let the police handle it."

"What if they don't get here in time?" Rocky said.

The three friends sat on the grass, and Pete sat under a bush, listening for the noisy truck. Piccolo heard it first, then Pete, and finally the humans. Mary ran inside to alert Mrs. Sunburg.

The truck rattled down the driveway, backed up to the pigpen, and stopped. The man got out, leaving the door open, as usual. Another man got out of the passenger side of the truck.

Pete immediately ran from the bush to the truck, but instead of going to the open door, he went underneath the truck and stayed behind a tire. He wanted to be certain neither of the men saw him before he jumped inside the truck.

He peered around the tire. Nobody was looking in his direction. Hogman was talking loudly and waving his hands around. The other man stood by the gate with a ring of keys. He was trying them on the lock, one at a time.

Pete crept along under the truck until he was beside the open door. He glanced out once more to be sure nobody was watching, then jumped onto the seat of the truck.

The box of pelts sat on the floor. Pete tentatively pawed at the one on top, moving it enough so that he could see underneath it. The next pelt was identical to the top one—sleek brown fur, soft and thick. A beaver? A mink? Pete wasn't sure what kind of animal the pelts were from.

Pete noticed a piece of paper lying on the floor beside the box. It said INVOICE across the top, followed by the name Bick Badgerton. Below that, scrawled in untidy handwriting, it said, "Nine beaver. Two rabbit. One fisher. Total due on delivery: $120.00."

I was right, Pete thought. Hogman is the trapper. He's killed and skinned all these animals, and now he's going to sell the pelts. Pete quickly did the division in his head, feeling sad. It came to only ten dollars per pelt. He thought the life of a wild creature with such beautiful fur should be worth more than ten dollars.

Pete's plan had been to sit in the truck and caterwaul until Alex came to get him, and then he would show Alex the pelts. Now he worried that Hogman might get back to the truck first, and then Alex would never see what was inside.

Pete had a better idea. He would take this invoice and one of the pelts and SHOW them to Alex. The humans always misunderstood what he told them, but they wouldn't be able to misunderstand this kind of evidence.

Pete sank his teeth into the top pelt and tried to drag it out of the box. It was heavier than he had anticipated. He braced his hind legs on the seat and tried again, but the pelt barely moved. He let go and pawed the first two pelts aside until he could see beneath them. He recognized the next pelt as a rabbit. He'd seen rabbits exactly like this one nibbling the grass in Alex's backyard, and it made him cringe to think of them caught in a cruel trap. Pete shuddered.

He looked at the pelt's four appendages, which had been the rabbit's narrow legs. Pete bit the pelt in the thinnest place, right above one of the rabbit's front feet. He bit as hard as he could, chewing and tugging until the whole rabbit's foot came off in his mouth.

He tried to spit it out, but he had clamped down so hard that the pelt above the foot was stuck on his teeth. As Pete pawed at the side of his mouth, he heard another vehicle pull up beside the truck. Curious, Pete peeked out the window.

A van had parked beside Hogman's truck. A woman holding a microphone and a man balancing a big camera on one shoulder got out of the van and walked toward the group by the pigpen.

"What's going on?" Hogman asked. "Who are you?"

"I'm Jenna Martinez, from channel four," the woman said. "I'm covering the pig story for the five o'clock news."

Hogman put his hands in front of his face. "No pictures," he said. "No comment. I don't want to be on TV."

Jenna turned to Alex. "Tell me what's happening," she said.

"This man was driving the truck when the pig fell off," Alex said. "Now he wants to take her back, even though the police gave custody to Foothills Animal Rescue, and they gave her to us."

Jenna stuck the microphone in Hogman's face. "Is that true?" she asked. "The pig fell off your truck?"

He backed away from her, keeping his face covered and shaking his head. "No comment," he said. "And no photos of me!"

"What's your name, sir?"

"That's none of your business, and if you put pictures of me on the air, I'll sue the station."

Pete quit watching while he tried to get the rabbit's foot unstuck from his teeth. Suddenly he realized the voices were getting louder. Hogman was coming toward the truck. If I'm going to take evidence, Pete thought, I need to take it now. With the rabbit's foot still hanging from the side of his mouth, he grabbed the invoice in his teeth, then jumped off the seat just as Hogman and the other man reached the two doors.

Pete dashed between Hogman's legs, his tail streaming out behind him. He hoped the cameraman was filming his daring escape.

"What was that?" the brother said. "An animal jumped out of your truck!"

"That fool cat was here again," Hogman said. Both men got in and slammed the doors. "He must belong to one of the kids or the old lady."

Keeping one hand in front of his face in case the camera pointed his way, Hogman yelled out the window: "I'll be back!" he shouted. To his brother, he added, "And next time I'll be armed!"

Pete ran into the woods behind Alex's house, then put the invoice in a thick clump of ferns where the wind couldn't blow it away. He didn't watch Hogman drive off; he didn't watch the TV people leave, either. He was too busy pawing at the rabbit's foot that was stuck in his mouth.

He pushed at it with his pink tongue. Yuck! He didn't like the taste, and he didn't want to cough up a hair ball made of rabbit fur. When the rabbit's foot finally came loose, he laid it on top of the invoice.

Then he took a complete cat bath, licking his shoulders and washing his face. Grooming himself calmed him. When he finished, he crept back to Mary's yard. The pig was asleep in her pen; Alex and the others had left.

Pete didn't want to put the rabbit's foot in his mouth again in order to carry it home. Too many pieces of fur had stuck to his tongue the first time.

He decided to leave the evidence where it was, and try to get Alex to follow him. If he howled loudly enough and acted distressed, Alex should get the hint and go see what Pete wanted to show him.

I'll sit on the steps and caterwaul, Pete decided, and when Alex opens the door, I'll run toward the clump of ferns.

Bick Badgerton drove his brother, Ram, to the gas station where Ram worked.

"I'll be off work at seven," Ram said. "If you want me to go back up there with you to get the pig, I can do it then."

"I'll have the pig long before seven," Bick said. "The slaughterhouse closes at six. As soon as I take this box of pelts to Ned, I'll go back and get the pig. By then that TV crew will be gone. I can't believe those kids got a reporter to drive all the way out there to take pictures of my pig."

"Maybe you ought to keep that pig," Ram said. "If she gets famous enough, you can sell pictures of her."

Bick looked at his brother as if he'd suddenly started speaking Chinese. "You're crazy," he said. "Who'd buy pictures of my pig?"

"She was already on the news once," Ram said, "and maybe she'll be on again today. I wouldn't want you to miss a chance for some easy money. A guy I heard about got two hundred dollars from one of the networks for a home video he took."

"Of a pig?"

"No, of Mount Saint Helens blowing its top."

"A volcano erupting is not the same as my pig lying in the dirt."

Ram shrugged. "You never know what's going to catch the public's attention," he said. "There are a lot of animal lovers out there. Maybe the pig will be a celebrity. You can make a pig Web page and sell hoofprints." He got out, then as Bick drove off, he called, "W-w-w dot p-i-g dot com!"

Don't listen to him, Bick told himself. Ram always had some get-rich-quick scheme, and not one of them had ever panned out. I shouldn't have involved him in the first place. I have a ramp for the truck and sturdy rope. I can lead the pig up the ramp by myself, the same as I did when I loaded her the first time.

He fumed while he drove the fifteen miles to Ned's shop. He had successfully avoided newspeople for seven years; he shouldn't have to confront them now in order to get his own pig back. He shouldn't have to put up with that snoopy cat prowling around in his truck, either. He shouldn't have to go through any of this hassle.

Drat those kids, anyway! This whole mess was their fault. If they had minded their own business and left his pig alone, none of this would have happened. The more he thought about it, the angrier he got. By the time he parked his truck in Ned's parking lot, he was steaming.

He picked up the box of pelts, then looked for the invoice. Where was it? He was positive he had laid it on the floor beside the box. Bick set the box on the roof of the truck while he looked under the seat. All he saw was an empty beer can, two old scratch-off lottery tickets with losing numbers, and the wrapper from yesterday's breakfast sandwich.

He went around to the driver's side and looked under that seat, too, in case the invoice had somehow slid over there, but the invoice wasn't under there, either.

Bick stomped into Ned's store and plopped the box down on the counter.

"I had an invoice ready for you," he said, "but it's gone. I gave my brother a ride to work; it must have fallen out of the truck when he got out. I have nine beaver, two rabbits, and a fisher. Total comes to one hundred twenty bucks."

"I can't pay you without an invoice," Ned said. "You know that." As he talked he picked up two pelts and looked at them. "What happened to this one?" he asked as he turned the fur over in his hands. "Looks like your dog took a bite out of it."

"I don't have a dog." Bick leaned closer. "Where?"

"Right there. One of the rabbit's front feet has been chewed off. That'll cut in half the amount I can pay you for it."

Bick grabbed the pelt in question and examined it. "That rabbit had all four feet when I put it in the box," he said. "You know I'm more careful than that. I wouldn't try to sell you a damaged pelt."

Ned shrugged. "You just did." He lifted each of the other pelts out of the box and looked them over carefully, as if expecting the others might also have missing parts.

Suddenly Bick slammed his fist on the counter, making Ned jump. "It was that cat!" he said.

"What cat?"

"Some kids stole my pig, and when I went to get her back, their cat got in my truck. He must have chewed on that rabbit pelt and ripped a foot off it."

Ned looked doubtful. "I suppose the cat took the invoice, too?"

"Maybe. Maybe he kicked it out accidentally, or maybe it stuck to his foot. How should I know? All I know is that me and my brother and that cat are the only ones who've been in my truck since I put the pelts and the invoice in there. Ram didn't chew off that rabbit's foot, and I sure didn't touch it, so that leaves the cat."

"Maybe you should go find that cat," Ned said. He started to laugh. "Ask him to return your invoice and your rabbit's foot."

"It isn't funny."

Ned struggled to quit smiling but lost the battle. "If the cat doesn't have your invoice, you can write up another one and send it to me. I'll mail you a check."

Bick shook his head. "I gotta have cash," he said. "Give me some paper and I'll make a new invoice now."

Ned took a lined yellow tablet from a drawer and handed it to Bick. "Just remember to only bill half for the rabbit that's missing a foot." He laughed some more. "Maybe the cat wanted a good-luck charm," he said.

"Ha. Ha." Bick wrote out the new invoice, collected his money, and left the shop. He'd find that cat, all right, and when he did, no good-luck charm on Earth would save the little thief.

8

As soon as the reporter and cameraman left, Mary unlocked the pigpen gate. She went in the pen, followed by Alex and Rocky.

Piccolo seemed glad to have company. She leaned against Alex's leg while the kids scratched behind her ears.

"I did some more Internet research about pigs this morning," Rocky said. "There's one really cool Web site that compares pigs to people. It said pigs are more like humans than any other animal is. Pig hearts, arteries, livers, and immune systems are like ours. So are their teeth!"

Alex squatted beside Piccolo, trying to see her teeth. Piccolo kept her mouth closed but pushed her snout toward Alex's face.

"Pigs get cancer and arthritis," Rocky continued, "and they respond to drugs much the same way people do."

"Gramma told me that when my great-uncle Fred had open heart surgery he got a pig's heart valve put in his heart," Mary said. "She said the mitral heart valves of pigs are grafted into human patients all the time. They last longer than man-made valves."

"I read about that," Rocky said. "Pig livers are used in humans, too, and pig cells have been used to treat diabetes."

Alex wondered how many pigs had given their lives so that sick people could have a new mitral heart valve or a liver transplant or some other life-saving treatment. Ordinarily, Alex was against using animals for research. His parents supported a group called Physicians Committee for Responsible Medicine that encouraged medical schools to use computer images instead of dogs and other animals in their laboratories. They also lobbied against cruel and unnecessary testing on animals for cosmetic products.

He thought about the ethics of using pig parts to save people. He wouldn't want Piccolo to be killed, but he wasn't sure how he would feel if someone in his family needed that kind of medical treatment. You can't get a liver from a computer.

Alex moved his fingers back and forth as he ran his hands down Piccolo's back, scratching her with his fingertips. Pete loved it when Alex did that to him, and the pig seemed to like it, too. Mary was right; this was a friendly, good-natured pig, and Alex was glad she had jumped off the truck and escaped.

"Gramma told me about a blind woman who has a trained pig instead of a Seeing Eye dog," Mary said. "She calls it her 'Seeing Eye hog' and says it's as efficient as a dog, and more visible."

"It would get noticed, that's for sure," Rocky said.

When Alex quit scratching the pig's back, Piccolo made low, grunting sounds and put her head under Alex's hand. He laughed, and massaged her some more.

Benjie came down the driveway and approached the pen. "I don't think they're going to show up," he said.

"Who?" Alex asked.

"The television people. I've been in my spy station watching for their truck."

"They came," Alex said. "They tried to interview Hogman, but he wouldn't talk to them. They left about ten minutes ago."

"They were here?" Benjie cried. "Why didn't you come get me?"

"I thought you knew. You said you were going to watch for them."

"I was! Were they driving a big truck with the station's letters on the side?"

"No. They were in a minivan. I don't think there was any sign on the door." Alex looked at Rocky. "Did you see a sign?"

"No," Rocky said.

"I was looking for a big truck," Benjie said. "What happened? Did they interview all of you?"

"Hogman got angry that they were here. He covered up

his face and threatened to sue the station if they put pictures of him on the news."

"Wow!" Benjie said. "I'll bet he's hiding from someone! Maybe he moved without paying his rent and that's why he doesn't want his picture taken. Maybe he murdered someone in another state!"

Alex smiled at his brother's inventive mind. No matter what happened, Benjie always had a theory about it. "Could be," Alex said.

"I should have stayed here," Benjie said. "I missed all the excitement. I saw Hogman's truck come and I saw him leave without Piccolo, but I stayed at my spy station 'cause I didn't want to miss the TV truck."

"Nothing much happened," Rocky told him. "The camera guy took some shots of Piccolo in her pen and we told about seeing her fall off the truck, and that was about it."

"The most action was when Pete got in Hogman's truck," Alex said. "It really made him angry when Pete jumped out of the truck and went tearing off."

"Pete practically knocked Hogman over when he ran between Hogman's legs," Mary said.

Alex and Mary laughed as they told about Pete, but Benjie looked worried. "Why did Pete go in the truck?" he asked.

"You know how curious he is. Maybe he smelled food inside."

"Remember when those burglars came to our house," Benjie said, "and Pete got in their truck and ate a bag of french fries and the burglars kidnapped him?"

"I remember," Alex said. "It was horrible."

"Pete should stay out of trucks," Benjie said, "especially when they belong to bad guys."

"I have to leave," Rocky said. "Mom's going to take me and Rufus to the off-leash dog park this afternoon."

"I'm going home, too," Alex said. "I promised I'd mow the lawn."

"Let's meet at five o'clock," Mary suggested, "and watch the news together, in case they show Piccolo."

"My house, five o'clock," Alex said, and everyone agreed.

When Alex and Benjie got home, Pete was waiting for them by the back door.

Alex held the door open for him, but instead of going in, Pete said, "Follow me!" and headed toward the ferns.

Benjie went inside.

Alex stood by the door, watching Pete.

The cat stopped partway across the yard and waited, looking back, as if expecting Alex to follow him.

Sometimes Alex wondered if Pete understood more than most cats do. It was uncanny, how Pete seemed to find important information and get Alex to notice it. It was almost as if Pete knew exactly what Alex's family and friends talked about and then tried to help them solve their problems.

That's ridiculous, Alex told himself. Pete was a great cat, but that's all he was: a cat. He was a bit more adventuresome than most cats, and he was certainly entertaining, the way he had cat fits and leaped to the top of the entertainment center, but Pete had no concept of life beyond his own small cat world.

When Alex didn't follow him, Pete trotted partway back to the house, stopped, and called again. "Come on, Alex, I have something to show you. I have evidence of a catastrophic crime."

"Get back here," Alex said. "I'm going in, and you'd better come in, too."

Pete put his nose in the grass, as if he were sniffing at something. Then he raised his head, looked at Alex, and caterwauled. The shrill noise brought Mrs. Kendrill to the door.

"What's wrong with Pete?" she asked.

Alex was already hurrying toward him. Before he got to where Pete was, Pete trotted farther away toward the clump of ferns.

Alex stopped. He examined the place Pete had sniffed, then looked toward the cat. "I'm not playing chase-the-cat," Alex said.

"Is Pete okay?" Mrs. Kendrill called.

"Yes. He wants me to play with him."

"I wish he would play more quietly," she said.

Alex turned away from Pete, and headed back to the house.

Disgusted, Pete followed. If Alex refused to look at Pete's important evidence, he might as well go inside, eat some crunchies, and take his nap.

Bick Badgerton filled his truck with gas, then pulled in to the drive-through line at Taco Time. It's a good thing Ned had let him make out a new invoice on the spot. He had been down to his last fifty cents, he was hungry, and the truck was running on fumes. If he hadn't been able to get cash for the pelts, he'd have been in big trouble.

Bick ordered his usual: a soft taco, a side of fries, and a large soda. Then, remembering that he'd had no breakfast, he changed his mind. Make that two tacos," he said. "With extra salsa."

He ate as he drove, thinking about the rabbit pelt that had been chewed. That thieving cat had cost him five dollars. Five bucks would have paid for his lunch. The more he thought about it, the more angry he got.

Soon his stomach was churning so much that he couldn't enjoy his food. He left the second taco and half of the fries lying on the seat.

Bick drove past Valley View Estates, past Hilltop, to the narrow road that led to the trailer he called home. It wasn't really his; Bick didn't know who actually owned it, but he had lived there for nearly two years now and nobody had noticed. The trailer sat well back in the woods, out of sight of the gravel road. It lacked indoor plumbing and electricity, but Bick didn't mind. A small wood-burning stove kept him warm in winter, and there was plenty of free firewood. The site was secluded, there was room for him to raise a few pigs, and best of all, it was free.

Bick parked in front of the trailer, went inside, and got his wire cutters. He also tucked a handgun into the top of his jeans. Then he returned to the truck to go after his pig. This time he planned to keep an eye out for that cat. If the cat got in Bick's truck again, it wouldn't be leaving on its own four feet.

What he'd really like to do is take a potshot at those smart-aleck kids who had stolen his pig, but he couldn't risk jail time. A cat was a different matter. The more he thought about it, the more Bick hoped the cat would come around and give him an excuse for some target practice.

He wondered if Ned had any market for cat pelts. That would be a fitting way to get revenge for the damaged rabbit skin, and pick up some extra money at the same time.

Rocky and Mary both arrived about fifteen minutes before five as Alex took popcorn out of the microwave and poured it into a big bowl. They all sat on the couch together.

Pete jumped into Alex's lap. He leaned his head toward the bowl, trying to get close enough to take a bite of popcorn.

"No, Pete," Alex said as he moved the bowl farther away. "You can't eat out of the bowl."

"I could if you didn't keep moving it," Pete said.

Alex lifted Pete off his lap and set the cat on the floor. Then he tossed one kernel of popcorn on the floor next to Pete.

Lizzy rushed over to see what it was, so Alex threw a piece of popcorn to her, too. Lizzy batted hers across the floor and chased it. Pete ate his, then asked for more.

"I've never been on TV," Mary said.

"Neither have I," Rocky said.

"We might not be on tonight, either," Alex said. "Not every story that they make gets used."

"Excuse me," Pete said. "One piece of popcorn is not nearly enough for a half-starved cat."

Alex tossed another kernel to Pete.

"Next time put more butter on it," Pete said.

The newscast started, and everyone turned their attention to the Kendrills' television set.

Everyone, that is, except Pete. He had thought of a new plan to show his evidence to the humans, and this was the perfect time to do it, while the kids were all together.

Pete had decided to retrieve only the invoice, and show it to the people. A piece of paper was easy to carry and it wouldn't leave fur in his mouth. Then, after they realized what he had brought them, he would get them to follow him to the fern grove, and show them the rabbit's foot.

Even though the humans are not as smart as cats are, he was certain they'd be able to figure out where Pete had gotten the rabbit's foot and the invoice.

All he needed now was a chance to slip out the door. It came when Mrs. Kendrill decided to empty the kitchen wastebasket. She opened the door, then left it open while she picked up the wastebasket and carried it to the garbage can, giving Pete plenty of time to bolt out the door, unseen.

He was running toward the ferns when he heard the noisy truck again. It had turned into Mrs. Sunburg's driveway. Pete stopped. What did Hogman intend to do now? Was he going to cut the pen wire and take Piccolo?

Instead of grabbing the invoice and carrying it home, Pete crept toward Mrs. Sunburg's yard. Pete considered running home and trying to get one of his family to come outside where they could see what was happening, but he knew from experience that whoever opened the door for him would invite him to come inside and, when he didn't, they would shut the door.

They couldn't see the pen or the truck from their doorway. It would be better, Pete decided, to watch Hogman so that he knew exactly what the man was doing.

Pete hunkered down under the bush closest to the pigpen. It's lucky for the people that I'm vigilant, he thought, since *none of them are on guard. It's a good thing I'm clever, coura-geous, and capable.*

He watched the truck stop next to Piccolo's pen.

Hogman got out of the truck, leaving the door open, as always. A tantalizing smell drifted out. Pete's nose twitched, and he leaned forward, trying to decide what it was. The odor was much stronger than the egg-and-cheese-sandwich smell had been, and it hinted of Mexican spices. Pete's pink tongue darted in and out. Did Hogman have enchiladas in his truck?

No! Pete told himself. You can't get distracted by food, no matter how good it smells. He wondered if the box of pelts was still on the floor of the truck. If it was, perhaps he could run back to the ferns now, and take only the invoice to Alex. He could easily carry the piece of paper, and when Alex saw what it was, he would follow Pete to the truck and find the whole box of animal pelts. Pete wouldn't have to put the rab-bit's foot in his mouth again.

Pete waited until Hogman's attention was on the locked gate. Then he dashed toward the truck, stood on his hind legs, and looked inside.

The box of pelts was gone—but something new had been added. A soft taco sat on the seat. Pete drooled when he saw it. He hardly ever got Mexican food because the humans thought it was too spicy for him. Pete loved cheese enchi-ladas. He loved bean burritos. Most of all, he loved soft tacos, and now there was a fresh taco sitting in plain sight, waiting to be eaten.

Pete glanced back at Hogman. The man's attention was focused on the fence. Pete knew better than to stay in the truck while he ate, but he thought he had time to jump up, grab the taco, and run. He would carry it to the ferns and, using extraordinary willpower, he would leave it there while he took the invoice to Alex. He would go back to eat it as soon as he'd accomplished his spy business.

Pete leaped onto the seat of the truck, then pressed his nose to the luscious-smelling taco. Oh, what bliss! This was cat heaven! He opened his jaws as wide as he could, clamped down on the middle of the taco, and tried to pick it up. When he lifted it, the filling tumbled out. Lettuce, cheese, tomato, and ground beef dropped onto the seat of the truck, and Pete was left with the empty tortilla in his mouth.

He couldn't carry the taco away when it was spilled all over the seat; he would have to eat it right now, in the truck. He crouched and began gulping the beef and cheese, gobbling it as quickly as he could. His mouth was full of taco meat when a hand clamped down on the back of Pete's neck.

"Gotcha!" Hogman said as he plopped down behind the wheel and slammed the truck door shut.

Pete tried to yell, "Let me go!" but his mouth was so full that it came out "Beleghmeeg!"

Hogman held on tight to Pete's fur as he started the engine and then drove the truck out Mrs. Sunburg's driveway and down Elm Lane to Valley View.

By the time they reached the corner of Valley View Drive and the main road, Pete had swallowed his mouthful of taco meat, and was caterwauling as loudly as he could.

He twisted and turned, clawing at Hogman's leg until the man let go of Pete's neck.

Pete scratched at the passenger-side window and yelled, "Help me! Let me out of here! I'm trapped!"

Hogman snorted. "You ain't goin' nowhere, cat," he said. "You've sneaked in my truck for the last time and chewed what doesn't belong to you."

Pete backed up to the opposite door, flattened his ears, and hissed at Hogman.

"Might as well save your breath. Ain't nobody going to hear you. We're going to take a nice little drive up the hill, but you won't be comin' down again." He patted the handgun that was tucked into his belt. "I'd do it right here, only I don't want to make more of a mess in my truck."

Pete looked at Hogman's gun, then at the man's expression. *He means it,* Pete thought. *He plans to drive me up the hill where no one can hear, and then he's going to shoot me.*

Pete's mind raced as the truck rattled through Hilltop and up the gravel road. He knew he needed to think of everything that could possibly happen, and decide how best to save himself.

If he pushed on the window handle, he could probably get the window open far enough to squeeze through—but there was no point trying to do that until the truck stopped. He'd only get hurt if he leaped from a moving vehicle, and then he'd be unable to run away.

My best chance of surviving this, Pete decided, is to act docile until he parks. If he gets out and leaves me in here, I'll open the window and jump.

If I can't do that, I'll let the man pick me up and take me out of the truck. Then, as soon as I'm out, I'll bite and claw and kick. He'll never be able to hold on. He'll drop me, and I'll run into the trees and escape.

Unless he shoots me before I reach the trees.

I should have stayed home, Pete thought. I could be lying on Alex's lap right now, listening to the news, and getting a kitty massage. I could be licking Lizzy's ears, or reading c-a-t words in the dictionary or catapulting to the top of the entertainment center. I could be eating buttered popcorn.

Instead here I am on a deserted country road with a man who wants to kill me.

Worst of all, nobody knows where I am. If I never come home again, Alex won't even know where to look for me.

9

"Piccolo's more interesting than traffic and weather," Alex said, halfway through the newscast. "Why don't they show her?"

Alex, Rocky, and Mary nibbled on the popcorn as they waited. They kept the newscast on, but the sound was turned down.

Suddenly the kitchen door banged open and Benjie rushed in, practically hysterical.

"Hogman kidnapped Pete!" he yelled.

"What?" Alex jumped to his feet.

"I was in my spy station, and I saw Hogman's truck go by, headed toward our street. I started to come home, to tell you, but before I got here the truck went past the other way, and Pete was in it! He was yowling and scratching at the window, trying to get out."

"Are you positive it was Pete?" Alex asked. "He was here just a few minutes ago, begging for popcorn."

"It was him," Benjie said. "Hogman took Pete!"

"Pete!" Alex called. "Here, Pete!" He began looking in all of Pete's favorite places. Lizzy was in her bed, but Pete's bed was empty. He wasn't under the table or on top of the entertainment center.

Alex ran upstairs to his room. Pete sometimes curled up on Alex's bed or sat on his desk. For some odd reason, the cat seemed to like being near the dictionary. He wasn't in any of those places. Alex checked the bedroom window; it was closed.

Alex ran back downstairs. "He's gone," he said. "I even looked under the beds, in case he was hiding."

"I thought he was in here with you," Mr. Kendrill said.

"He was," Alex said. "He tried to eat the popcorn."

"Then how did he get out?"

"I don't know," Alex said, "but he isn't here now."

"Honestly," Mrs. Kendrill said, "I've never known an animal that was such an escape artist. If he isn't sneaking out the door, he's going out the upstairs window."

"He's in Hogman's truck!" Benjie wailed. "I saw him. Hogman stole Pete!"

"Why would he do that?" Mrs. Kendrill said.

"Pete jumped in his truck earlier," Rocky said, "and the guy got angry. He acted as if he doesn't like cats, so why would he steal one?"

"Maybe Pete got in the truck again and Hogman didn't

see him," Mr. Kendrill said. "Remember that time at our old house when Pete got in the FedEx truck and rode two blocks to the next stop before the driver noticed him?"

"This driver would have heard him," Benjie said. "Pete was yowling and clawing at the window."

"Maybe he took Pete on purpose," Mary said, "because he was angry that we have his pig."

Benjie cried harder. "He's going to throw Pete in the river!" he sobbed. "Or he'll drive really fast, like he did with Piccolo, and make Pete fall out."

"More likely he'll turn him loose in the woods," Mrs. Kendrill said.

Alex and Rocky spoke at the same time: "The trap!"

Alex thought of the cruel trap he'd seen in the woods. If Pete was scared, he'd run without looking where he was going. Alex shuddered.

"Let's not panic," Mr. Kendrill said. "Maybe we can find him. Benjie, which way did the truck go?"

"Up the hill. Toward Hilltop."

"Toward the woods," Alex said. "Toward the trap."

"I'll drive up that way," Mr. Kendrill said. "Maybe I can catch up to the truck. Or if he's let Pete go, we might be able to spot him." He grabbed his car keys from the hook by the back door.

Mrs. Kendrill turned off the oven and the TV. "I'll go with you," she said.

"Me, too," Alex said. "If Pete's been let out somewhere, he's most likely to come if he hears my voice."

"I'm coming, too," Benjie said. "I want to help find Pete."

"Do you want me to stay here?" Rocky asked. "I could let Pete in if he comes back."

"That would be great," Alex said. "Thanks."

"I'll go around the neighborhood," Mary said, "and alert everyone to watch for Pete."

The Kendrills piled into their car. Mr. Kendrill drove while the others peered out the windows, hoping to see a big brown-and-white cat.

Mr. Kendrill drove to the main road, past Benjie's spy station, then turned out of Valley View Estates and headed up the hill toward Hilltop. He drove slowly through the small village and out the other side, going up the gravel road where the kids had seen Piccolo fall from the truck.

Benjie rolled down his window and hollered, "Here, Pete! Here, Pete!"

Alex knew the cat would never approach a moving vehicle, but he didn't say so. If it made Benjie feel better to call Pete, let him do it.

Regret settled on Alex's shoulders like a heavy coat. This is partly my fault, he thought. I've never let Pete out on purpose, but I haven't been strict enough with him about staying inside. When Pete sneaked out, it was easier to ignore him than to chase after him and take him back home. Pete had made it clear that he liked going outdoors, and I've allowed him to get away with it.

I should have walked him on the leash more, to keep him happy, Alex thought, and then made sure he stayed in the rest of the time. I should have kept him safe. Pete's a smart cat, but he can't understand all of the dangers that could befall him. Alex feared that Mary was right. Curious Pete had gone in the truck, and when Hogman saw the cat there, he got angry and drove off, taking Pete with him. Alex leaned his forehead against the cool window glass. He couldn't bear to think of Pete in the clutches of that awful man.

"Pete must have sneaked out when I emptied the kitchen wastebasket," Mrs. Kendrill said. "I left the door open while I went out to the garbage can. I never saw Pete, but you know how he bolts sometimes when he sees the open door."

Alex felt a tiny bit better, knowing his mom recognized how often Pete tried to run out. He could tell she felt guilty, too.

"It isn't your fault, Mom," Alex said. "Pete has sneaked out on all of us from time to time no matter how alert we are."

Mrs. Kendrill gave Alex a grateful smile.

"I'm going to pull off at the next wide spot," Mr. Kendrill said, "so that we can get out and call Pete. If Pete was yowling and trying to escape, the man might have turned him loose as soon as he reached the woods."

He pulled the car onto a wide shoulder area, and stopped the engine. Everyone got out.

"Stay on the road," Mr. Kendrill said. "Cats have excellent hearing. Pete will hear us if he's anywhere nearby."

"Here, Pete!" Alex called. "Here, kitty, kitty!"

"Petey! Petey!" Benjie hollered. "Come, Sweetey Petey!"

When they stopped calling, straining to hear an answering meow, they heard only the whisper of the leaves rubbing together in the breeze, and the crunch of gravel underfoot as they walked along the road.

Alex felt sick to his stomach. What if Pete never came back? What if he never saw his cat again and never found out what had happened to him? It would be sad to lose Pete under any circumstances, but it would be horrible to lose him and not know what happened to him. Pet cats are supposed to live to an old age, to be pampered and taken care of. They aren't supposed to be kidnapped. They aren't supposed to vanish when they're still young and healthy.

If I don't find him, Alex thought, how will I stand the uncertainty?

"Let's drive on up the road," Mr. Kendrill said. "We'll stop again at the next turnout."

At the next wide spot, they stopped again. They called,

looked, listened, then called some more, but they didn't see or hear Pete.

"Maybe we should go all the way to the end of the road," Alex said, "and then, if we don't find the truck, we can stop at the turnouts on our way back down."

"Good plan," his dad replied.

"Petey!" Benjie bellowed one last time as he headed back to the car. "Here, Sweetey Petey!"

Pete felt the truck slow, and saw the man steer it to the right. Pete raised his head to look out the window. The man was stopping at a wide spot on the side of the road. There were no houses nearby, no people, nothing but forest.

No one would hear a gunshot in this remote place. No one would find a dead cat on the side of the road.

The man stopped the engine and opened the door on his side, keeping an eye on Pete. He slid the small gun out of the top of his pants and clicked off the safety latch.

"I hope you enjoyed my taco, cat," he said, "seeing as it was the last meal you'll ever eat."

Holding the gun in his right hand, he reached across the seat with his left hand. For a second, Pete thought the man intended to shoot him then, but instead the man grabbed Pete's front legs with his left hand and used his right hand, which still held the gun, to push on Pete's backside as he moved Pete toward him.

Pete did not resist. He went limp and let the man slide him across the seat toward the open door. He hoped his plan would work. Could he fight hard enough to make Hogman drop him? Even if he did, could Pete run fast enough to hide in the woods before Hogman could take aim and fire the gun?

The trees were only about ten yards from the truck, but ten yards is a lot of ground to cover when a person's aiming a gun at you. Maybe he could zigzag as he ran, make himself a more difficult target.

Get ready to fight, Pete told himself. As soon as I'm out of this truck, the mighty warrior cat will go into attack mode.

Hogman stood close to the seat of the truck as he pulled Pete toward him, blocking the exit in case Pete tried to bolt out the door. When Pete reached the edge of the seat, the man scooped him up, then quickly backed away from the truck. Still grasping Pete's front legs, he tried to maneuver the gun so that it pointed at Pete's head.

The cat who had been obedient a moment earlier now acted as if all of Catdom was depending on him to defeat his captor. Pete twisted and turned, ducking his head from side to side and thrashing his tail. He stuck out his back toenails as he kicked at the man.

"Hold still!" the man demanded. He put his forearm next to Pete's head, trying to keep Pete from turning his head away from the gun.

Pete bit the man, hard, just above his wrist. At the same

time, he kicked with his hind legs, claws extended, catching the hand that held the gun.

Hogman swore and struggled to position the gun. Pete bit the man's arm again, sinking his teeth in farther this time. The man yelped and jerked away, loosening his grasp on Pete's front legs.

With his front paws finally free, Pete clawed at the man's face, leaving deep scratches on both cheeks. The man grabbed Pete around the middle, shoved him into the crook of his arm, and squeezed so hard that Pete thought he might break in two.

The man raised the gun.

Pete thrust his hind foot toward the gun, hoping to spoil the man's aim. His foot came down on the trigger.

BANG!

The sound exploded, echoing through the forest.

10

As Alex returned to the car he heard a gun-shot.

Alex gasped; Mrs. Kendrill covered her mouth as she screamed. They all stood still, listening, but no more shots rang out.

"The meanie Hogman shot Petey!" Benjie said, and began to cry.

"Maybe he missed," Mr. Kendrill said. "Maybe Pete ran away."

"If he had missed," Alex said, "he would have fired the gun again." They all hurried into the car. Alex felt cold, as if he'd been plunged into an icy stream. His hands shook as he pulled the door shut.

Beside him, Benjie cried harder. "I want Petey," he said.

"Let's go," Mr. Kendrill said.

"That shot was close by," Mrs. Kendrill said, as the car moved forward. "He can't be far ahead of us."

They continued uphill but had gone only a short distance when Hogman's truck came speeding around the curve toward them. The truck swerved erratically across the center of the road as if the driver wasn't paying attention.

Mr. Kendrill pulled to the side, leaning on the horn. The truck jerked back into its own lane and kept going.

"Stop!" Alex yelled. Mr. Kendrill honked the horn again.

As the truck clanked past them, spewing gravel out behind it, Alex saw the driver. His face was contorted in anger and streaked with blood. He didn't even glance at the Kendrills as he steered the truck downhill.

Mr. Kendrill read the truck's license number out loud, and Mrs. Kendrill wrote it down.

"I didn't see Pete," Alex said. "If he's still in the truck, he—he can't stand up and claw at the window." Alex tried to swallow the lump that seemed stuck in his throat.

"I don't think he's in the truck anymore," Mrs. Kendrill said sadly. "I think we need to look for him up ahead."

Mr. Kendrill drove slowly up the hill.

Alex stared at the side of the road, watching for a lump of brown-and-white fur, hoping he wouldn't see it.

Mr. Kendrill had driven only a short way beyond the curve when he saw another spot wide enough to pull off. He stopped the car again.

"I don't see Pete," Mrs. Kendrill said. "Maybe he really did get away."

"Or maybe we haven't yet come to where the shot was fired," Mr. Kendrill said.

With his heart in his throat, Alex got out of the car. "Pete?" he called. "Pete, where are you?"

Benjie got out, too, but instead of calling for Pete, he pointed at the gravel and began to cry even harder. "Blood!" he said.

Alex looked at the crimson drops that splattered the side of the road. Benjie was right.

Mr. Kendrill put his index finger on one of the drops, then wiped his finger on his handkerchief.

"It's fresh," he said.

Mrs. Kendrill put her arms around the sobbing Benjie.

"Petey's dead!" Benjie wailed.

"Maybe not," Alex said. "If the shot had killed him, he would be lying here. Maybe Pete only got wounded, and he ran away and hid."

"Maybe meanie Hogman took Petey with him," Benjie said.

"I doubt it," Mr. Kendrill said. "If Pete was bleeding, it would make a mess in the truck. Why would the man do that?"

"He might take Pete so we couldn't find him," Alex said.

"When he left this spot, he didn't know we were following him," Mrs. Kendrill said. "He would have thought nobody heard the gunshot."

"He's hiding the evidence," Benjie said. "He's going to bury Pete."

"Anyone who would kill a family pet wouldn't bother to bury the body," Mr. Kendrill said.

"The man had blood on his face when he went past us," Alex said.

Benjie quit bawling. "He did?"

"Yes. There were big streaks of blood on his cheeks."

"Maybe Hogman didn't shoot Pete," Benjie said. "Maybe Pete shot Hogman!"

Alex thought it highly unlikely that Pete could have done that, but he kept quiet. Let Benjie cling to his hope.

"Let's search this area," Mr. Kendrill said, "but if we don't find Pete quickly, I think we should go back home and call the police."

"Pete!" Alex called over and over. "Here, Pete!"

After seeing the blood on the side of the road, Alex felt even more desperate to find Pete. He imagined what had happened, clearly seeing the man aiming at Pete, shooting, hitting the cat but not killing him. He envisioned Pete, dripping blood but able to run away before the man could get off a second shot.

He pictured Pete, bleeding and weak, hiding alone in

the woods, too scared and feeble to move. I have to find him, Alex thought. I have to!

Starting where the blood was, Alex walked in an ever larger circle, thinking he might see another drop of blood that would be a clue to which direction Pete had gone. He saw only the gravel road and then the prickly leaves of Oregon grapes and the graceful stems of sword ferns leading into the cedar, fir, and alder trees.

Darkness comes early in the deep woods, as the sun vanishes behind the tall trees. While the Kendrills searched through the thick undergrowth, dusk settled over the forest. The woods that seemed peaceful with sunlight filtering through the open spaces between trees now took on a menacing look.

Alex shivered. He wouldn't want to spend the night alone out here. He didn't want Pete spending the night out here, either. There were probably coyotes and cougars, and huge owls with sharp claws and night-vision eyes. If Pete was already injured, he wouldn't be able to run fast or put up a fight, and a predator might smell blood, and track him down.

Alex called Pete's name over and over, but there was no answering "meow"—no sign of the big brown-and-white cat.

"It's getting dark," Mrs. Kendrill said.

"We need to go home," Mr. Kendrill said, "and call the

police. Now that we have a license number, they can see who owns that truck. They can question him, and maybe find out what he did with Pete."

Alex didn't want to leave. What if Pete was hiding somewhere, alone in the dark forest? But Alex did want to let the police know what happened.

"I'll be glad when cellular phone service comes out this far," Mrs. Kendrill said. "If we had a cell phone, we could have called the police as soon as we saw the truck pass us."

"After we contact the police," Alex said, "can we come back up here? We could bring flashlights and keep looking."

"Let's see what the police say before we decide that," Mr. Kendrill said.

Alex got in the car. Benjie huddled beside him, sniffling.

"Will you be able to find this spot again?" Mrs. Kendrill asked, "or do we need to mark it somehow?"

"It's the third wide space after the gravel starts," Mr. Kendrill said. "I'll find it."

Alex closed his eyes as the car turned around and headed downhill. I'll be back, Pete, he promised silently. I'll be back, and I'll keep looking until I find you.

11

A split second after *the shot rang out, Hogman dropped Pete. Pete landed on his paws and took
off toward the trees. In his panic, Pete forgot his plan to
zigzag; instead he galloped straight for the woods, expecting
another shot at any second. Pete's ears echoed from the gunshot, and his front legs and stomach ached where the man
had held him too tight, but fear gave him strength and speed.*

*Even after he reached the trees, Pete kept running. Afraid
that the man would chase him and take aim, Pete pushed
through the forest, ignoring the prickly bushes and vines that
snagged his fur, and paying no attention to which way he
was going. He climbed over fallen trees, squeezed between
crowded seedlings, and scrambled through a patch of
thistles.*

*He jumped over an anthill, barely avoided a clump of poi-
son oak, and badly scratched one ear when he misjudged how
close he was to a blackberry thicket. He didn't care where he*

was or how far he went. All he wanted was to put as much distance as possible between himself and the man with the gun.

When he had run until he felt on the verge of collapse, Pete chose the highest tree he could see and climbed up the trunk. His claws dug into the rough bark as he went higher and higher, shoving his head and shoulders through the leaves.

At last, too tired to climb one more inch, he crawled out on a horizontal limb and stopped. His sides heaved from exertion, but except for that he lay completely still, listening, afraid he would hear Hogman's heavy boots pursuing him. He heard only the soft cooing of a mourning dove high in the treetop above him.

After a few minutes with no indication that the man was nearby, Pete peered down. The ground was a long way below his branch. He hadn't realized he had climbed this high. He was much higher than when he sneaked out Alex's bedroom window and went down the maple tree.

Looking down, Pete felt dizzy. He dug his claws into the branch and stared straight ahead. He'd never be able to climb down again by himself. He would have to stay in the tree and hope Alex found him.

Pete was exhausted, but he didn't dare close his eyes. He couldn't take a chance on going to sleep, because if he fell asleep, he might drop off the branch. He had survived the *furious Hogman with a gun; now he needed to keep his wits about him until he got rescued.*

He wondered why Hogman had not come after him. He hadn't even fired at Pete as Pete ran toward the woods, though there would have been a few seconds when Pete was still visible.

Maybe he couldn't chase me, Pete thought. Maybe when the gun went off, the bullet hit him by mistake. That idea made Pete blink his blue eyes in surprise. He had felt his foot hit something hard, like metal, a split second before the loud noise. Had it been the trigger? Had he shot the man who was trying to shoot him?

Pete thought it over and decided that must be what had happened. If so, he hoped the man wasn't badly hurt. No matter how much he disliked Hogman, he didn't want to kill the man.

Pete would not have intentionally shot anyone. He had never even seen an actual gun before, although he'd seen them on television. Cats and other animals didn't have weapons. Only humans used such barbaric devices.

If I shot him, it was self-defense, Pete thought. I didn't shoot him on purpose. I was struggling to get away when my foot accidentally hit the trigger.

As Pete bolted away from the noise of the gunshot, Bick doubled over in pain, pressing his hand to his thigh. When he took his hand away, he saw blood on his fingers. A red spot oozed on the side of his pants leg and dripped onto the road.

Bick couldn't believe it. The cat had shot him! While he was trying to point the gun at the cat's head, the cat's foot had pressed down on the trigger, the gun had gone off, and the bullet had grazed Bick in the leg.

Furious, he kicked at the gravel, then groaned when the swift motion sent a sharp stab of pain up to his hip. Gingerly, he felt the wound again; he supposed he would need stitches. Maybe even surgery. He'd have to drive himself to the hospital emergency room and get help.

Bick hated doctors! He punched his fist down on the hood of the truck. There would be endless paperwork, and it would probably cost him an arm and a leg, but he couldn't leave a gunshot wound untreated and risk infection.

He wasn't going to admit that a cat had pulled the trigger, though. He'd tell the doctor that the gun had gone off accidentally as he was putting it in his holster. He'd say the wound was self-inflicted. The doc might laugh at him for that, but not as hard as he'd laugh if Bick admitted he'd been shot by a cat. He wouldn't tell anyone, not even his brother, what had really happened. If he did, he'd never hear the end of it.

Bick threw the handgun on the floor of the truck and

got behind the wheel. He wished he had an automatic transmission; that leg was going to kill him every time he let the clutch in or out. Bick gritted his teeth, pushed in on the clutch, and started the engine, cursing the cat as he did.

Bick shifted into gear and steered with one hand, keeping his left hand pressed against the bloodstain on his thigh, to try to stanch the bleeding. The leg throbbed now, and Bick pushed harder on the gas pedal, crossing the center line as he went around the first curve.

A horn blasted. Bick tensed and swerved back to the right. There was never any traffic up here, and the sudden noise startled him. The horn honked again as Bick sped past, and he heard someone yell, "Stop!"

Was it that same kid, the one who had stolen his pig? The one with the cat? Bick couldn't tell and he sure as heck wasn't going to stop to find out. What would that kid be doing up here, anyway? He couldn't be looking for his cat because nobody had seen Bick drive off with it.

He winced as the pain shot up his leg again. He wished now that he'd shoved the cat out of the truck and left him next to the pigpen instead of driving away with him. But how was he to know that the cat was capable of causing so much trouble?

Bick removed his hand from his thigh and gingerly touched his face. He could tell that the places where the cat had scratched him were beginning to scab over, but both cheeks still stung and he'd probably have scars.

Muttering under his breath about what he would do to that cat if he ever saw him again, Bick drove past Hilltop, past Valley View Estates, and down the hill toward the outskirts of Seattle. He followed the blue hospital signs until he reached the closest hospital. Leaving his truck across the street, Bick limped in the emergency entrance.

"I need to see a doctor," he told the admitting clerk. "I accidentally shot myself in the leg."

"How bad is it?" the clerk asked. "Do you need help right away?"

"I ain't waiting till tomorrow, if that's what you mean," Bick said.

"How did you get here?"

"I drove."

The clerk nodded. "If you drove unassisted, it's not a critical emergency," she said. "Please sit here and fill out these forms." She handed Bick a clipboard that had several pieces of paper attached.

"No need for a lot of paperwork," Bick said. "I don't have insurance."

"I need the information anyway."

Bick hesitated. For a minute he considered walking out the door and going home, but his leg hurt too much and he was worried about blood poisoning or even gangrene.

He sat down and began filling in the blanks, making things up as he went.

Name: Brock Thorsen. Social security number: don't have it with me. Bick used his brother's address and phone number, changing one digit of each. For employer, he wrote "self-employed farmer." He continued down the page, inventing whatever information he needed. By the time the hospital figured out that he'd made it all up, his leg would be patched up and he'd be out of there.

When he got to the line that asked why he needed treatment, he put "gunshot wound in leg." Under explanation he added "My gun went off accidentally." Then he handed the papers back to the clerk.

In a few minutes a nurse called, "Brock Thorsen," and Bick followed her into an examining room. Her name badge said Rosemary. Handing him a hospital gown, she said, "Ties go in the back. Pull the curtain open when you've changed." She pulled the curtain closed and walked away.

Bick dropped his blood stained pants and looked at the hole in his thigh. It still hurt like crazy, but it didn't look as deep as he had feared. The bleeding had slowed to an ooze. Maybe he wouldn't need surgery, after all. A few stitches and he'd be good as new.

He slipped his arms into the hospital gown and tied the strings behind his neck. It was a good thing he'd left his underpants on; this skimpy gown wouldn't cover a small boy, much less a grown man.

Bick pulled the curtain open and sat on the bed with his legs dangling over the side.

"Those are some wicked-looking scratches," Nurse Rosemary said when she returned. She reached for Bick's face as if she were going to touch them. "What happened?"

"Oh, those are from the blackberry bushes," Bick said as he leaned away from her. "I was pruning them. I ain't here for the scratches; I'm here because I got shot in the leg." What good was it, Bick thought, to write down exactly what had happened and what treatment you needed if they weren't gong to read what you wrote?

The nurse bent over, and peered at Bick's thigh. "Who shot you?" she asked.

"I did. It was an accident. I was putting my gun away and I thought it was empty."

Rosemary nodded. "Put your feet up on the bed," she said. "It will help slow the bleeding."

As he did that, she lifted Bick's wrist and looked at the bite marks on his arm. "What happened here?" she asked.

"What?"

"Looks like you got bit."

"Oh, that. You don't have to do anything about that. All I want is for you to take care of my leg where I got shot."

"Right," the nurse said. She let go of Bick's arm, but she looked again at his face. "They must have been huge blackberry bushes," she said.

He was getting seriously annoyed with this woman. Why was she fussing about a few scratches on his face and arm when he had taken a bullet in his leg? A person could bleed to death in this place while the nurse yammered on about blackberry bushes.

"Forget the scratches," Bick said. "I just want my leg fixed."

"The doctor will be here in a couple of minutes," Rosemary said.

She left, pulling the curtain closed behind her. For most patients, Rosemary would write her assessment of the patient's condition on the chart and leave it for the doctor while she went on to the next patient. But something about this case bothered her. Those scratches on the man's face were too deep to be caused by a wayward blackberry bush. There were several of them on both cheeks, and more on his arms, as if someone with long fingernails had been fighting for her life.

The bite marks were deep, too. They weren't made by human teeth, but it's possible that a person's small dog had tried to defend her from attack. It seemed likely to Rosemary that this man had tangled with a person, not a blackberry bush. Maybe he was lying about the gunshot, as well. Perhaps it had not been accidental.

Still, if someone had shot him, why would he try to protect that person's identity? Unless he had been the shooter and had somehow injured himself along with the other person. Clearly, he had struggled with someone.

Rosemary explained her concerns to the doctor on duty and then, following hospital protocol for any suspected crime, she called the police.

Sgt. Donald Skyler was on telephone duty at the police station when Rosemary called. She identified herself and explained why she was calling. "I'm pretty sure he's lying about how his face got scratched," she said, "and there are bite marks on his arm."

"I haven't had any reports of an assault," Sgt. Skyler said.

"The bite marks aren't from a person. They look as if it might have been a small dog, or even a cat."

"Can you get him to stay at the hospital for a while?" he asked.

"He isn't going anywhere," Rosemary replied. "He's waiting for one of the emergency-room doctors to look at his leg wound."

"Keep him waiting," Sgt. Skyler said. "I'll send an officer over to question him."

12

Bick shifted on the bed in the emergency-room cubicle, trying to get comfortable. His leg hurt, and no matter which way he positioned it, he couldn't ease the pain. The scratches hurt, too, and his arm ached where the cat had bit him.

I need a Tylenol, Bick thought, or maybe even some codeine. What was taking so long? Once he'd been called in from the waiting room and had donned this foolish shorty nightgown and had seen the nurse, he thought his wait was over. He expected the doctor to come through the opening in the curtain at any minute, but he didn't come. The nurse didn't return, either. With the high price of emergency-room care, you'd think the service would be better.

Bick wasn't used to waiting. For that matter, he wasn't used to sitting around doing nothing. He drummed his fingers on the edge of the bed. He lay down, then sat up again. Once, he stood and poked his head through the curtain opening and looked out, but all he saw was the nurses station, void of nurses.

At first Bick was annoyed; then he got angry. Was he being ignored because he didn't have insurance? Was he some kind of second-class citizen?

His anger turned to anxiety. What if they were checking what he'd written on the admissions paper? What if they had figured out that he'd given false information? What if they were calling the cops?

I shouldn't have come here, Bick decided. Hospitals were no good; the people asked too many nosy questions that were none of their business. Why did they need his telephone number in order to sew up his leg? What did it matter if his family had a history of cancer? He wasn't here for chemo; he was here to get the hole in his leg closed up. By the time they got around to helping him, he'd have to change the age he'd put on their paper because he'd be a year older.

He looked closely at the wound in his leg. If he cleaned it out good, put some antiseptic on it, then covered it with gauze and held the sides shut with tape, it would probably heal without leaving too big of a scar. He should have done that in the first place. He should have gone straight home and taken care of his own problem.

Never trust anyone. That had been Bick's motto all his life, but he'd never had to apply it to a hospital before.

Bick picked up his pants, grimacing as he moved. The wound might be treatable on his own, but it still hurt like crazy. Before he could step into his pants, the curtain parted and a police officer entered followed by Nurse Rosemary.

"Brock Thorsen?" the officer said.

Bick looked around, as if wondering who the officer was talking to.

The officer pointed at Bick. "Are you Brock Thorsen?"

"Oh," Bick said. "Oh, yeah, that's me, but I've decided not to wait for the doctor. It's taking too long, and I'm tired. I'm leaving; I'll take care of the leg myself."

"You shouldn't do that," Rosemary said. "Your leg might need stitches. You can't treat it yourself."

"Well, nobody around here is fixing it. I got better things to do than sit here and twiddle my thumbs."

"The doctor will be here shortly," Rosemary said. "Please lie down and keep your feet up. You make the bleeding worse when you stand."

The police officer said, "Officer Dingam, Hilltop Police Department. I have some questions for you before you go."

"You got the wrong person. You must be looking for the guy in the next bed."

"I don't think so."

"There's no reason to be questioning me; I haven't done anything wrong."

"Then you won't mind answering a few questions."

Bick sat down, not looking at the officer. "About what?"

"How did you get those scratches on your face?"

"What do you care? It's illegal to get scratched?"

"Answer the question."

"I already told the nurse. I was pruning some blackberry vines when one of them scratched me."

"Right."

"They were big prickly vines; got me right in the face."

"More than once," the officer said. "You'd think after one deep scratch like that, you'd stay away from the blackberries."

Bick glared at the man but said nothing.

"Who bit you on the arm?"

Bick looked at the teeth marks, still clearly visible on his arm. "I was playing with my dog, wrestling around, you know, but he got a little carried away. No harm done."

"A dog's teeth are bigger than that."

"It's a little dog," Bick said.

Officer Dingam nodded. The bite wounds clearly had not been inflicted by a person, but he doubted any dog was that small. Looked more like cat bites to him, which would make sense given the scratches.

He'd never heard of a cat defending its owner against an attacker, although he supposed it was possible. But what about the gunshot? No dog or cat could have done that. This man's story did not compute. He was lying about the blackberries and lying about the dog. The question was, why? What was he hiding?

Frustrated by the man's attitude and the lack of information, Officer Dingam said, "Thanks for your time," and left the room

While Officer Dingam had been questioning Bick, Sgt. Skyler received a call from Mr. Kendrill. An experienced officer, Sgt. Skyler had heard his share of wacky reports from the public, but he didn't remember ever getting a call regarding a kidnapped cat. He was about to suggest that the caller contact the humane society when Mr. Kendrill got to the part about hearing a gunshot.

"Within a minute or two of the gunshot, we saw the man we were looking for go past us in his truck," Mr. Kendrill said. "He was headed back toward town, driving erratically, and there was blood on his face. We yelled at him to stop, but he kept going. We went farther up the road and found blood splattered on the shoulder. We looked for our cat there, but we didn't find him."

Sgt. Skyler sighed. He detested animal cruelty cases almost as much as he hated to hear about abused children. What was wrong with people who took out their anger on little kids or helpless animals? They were sickos, that's what they were. Sickos.

It made his ulcer flare to think of somebody snatching a family's pet cat, driving off with it, and then shooting the cat in cold blood. He wrote down the truck's license number, the location where the man had been seen, and the cat owner's name, address, and phone number. He also took a description of the truck's driver.

"I'll get back to you as soon as I have anything to report," he said, but realistically he didn't think it was likely to be anytime soon, if ever. There were so many crimes committed every day and the police force was stretched so thin that he knew no one would have time to devote to a kidnapped cat.

Sometimes Sgt. Skyler thought he was in the wrong business. Maybe he should quit and find work that didn't get him emotionally churned up.

He was still fretting over the missing cat when Officer Dingam checked in. "I'm leaving the hospital," Dingam said. "The man in emergency is lying about how he got hurt, but I don't know why. I can't pin anything on him. He gave his name as Brock Thorsen; see if you can find any record on him. I don't know how he got shot. He has scratches and bite marks that look as if he tangled with a cat, but he won't admit that. There's something fishy about the whole scene."

When he heard the word "cat," Sgt. Skyler stiffened. "What's this guy look like?" he asked.

As Officer Dingam described the hospital patient, Sgt. Skyler looked at the notes he had jotted down from Mr.

Kendrill's phone call. Medium height, fiftyish, in need of a shave and a haircut. Looks as if he rarely showers.

It was him, all right. No doubt about it. Sgt. Skyler would bet last month's salary that the man at the hospital had been scratched and bitten by the kidnapped cat. Quickly he told Officer Dingam about Pete and about the gunshot that the Kendrills had heard.

"I ran the truck's license number through the computer," he said. "It's registered to a Bick Badgerton."

"I'm returning to the emergency room," Officer Dingam said.

Rosemary saw him approach the entrance to the cubicle, and waved him in.

"Not you again," Bick said.

"I want another look at those bites," Officer Dingam said.

"Haven't you got any criminals to track down? You got nothing to do but harass law-abiding citizens?"

"What kind of dog did you say you have?"

"A little one."

"Those look like cat bites to me," the officer said.

"I don't have a cat."

"Maybe it wasn't your own cat."

Rosemary saw a flicker of fear in her patient's eyes, and she knew the police officer was on the right track. This man had been scratched and bitten by a cat, but he didn't want them to know it.

"Did you know that cat scratches can be dangerous?" Rosemary asked.

"Huh?"

"Cat scratches are full of bacteria, and a bite is even worse. There have been several cases where people got bit by a cat, and the bite became badly infected. I know of one patient who died."

"Someone died from a cat bite?" Bick looked closely at his wrist.

"It would surely be too bad if a person walked out of a hospital without getting treatment for something that's potentially lethal," Officer Dingam said, "just because that person didn't want to admit he'd been bitten by a cat."

Bick was silent, thinking it over. "What makes you think I got scratched and bit by a cat?" he asked.

"Cats scratch their adversaries, but dogs don't usually defend themselves with their toenails," Officer Dingam said. "Also, those marks on your arm look more like cat bites than dog bites," he said. "You want to tell me about that cat?"

"Look, I came in to get help for a leg wound," Bick said, "not to get questioned by the cops." He glared at Rosemary. "You must be the one who called the cops. Why'd you do that? Where's the doctor?"

"He'll be in soon," Rosemary said, ignoring his other question.

"If you don't want to discuss the bites, tell me about that leg wound," the officer said, but Bick shook his head.

"I already told the admitting clerk," he said, "and I told the nurse. If a doctor wants to come and stitch me up, right now, I'll tell him. Otherwise, I'm out of here." He stood and reached for his pants.

Officer Dingam turned to Rosemary. "Would you please see if the doctor is ready to examine Mr. Thorsen?" he asked.

She hurried out, returning almost immediately with a doctor.

"I'm Dr. Fleming," he said. "While I take a look at your leg, Mr. Thorsen, suppose you tell me exactly what happened to you."

Bick sighed loudly, as if this were a huge imposition, then lay back on the table again. While the doctor probed the area on Bick's thigh, Bick repeated the story about accidentally shooting himself while he was putting the gun in its holster.

"I need to clean this wound," the doctor said.

"Then do it," Bick said. "I've been here too long already."

"Are you right-handed or left-handed?" Officer Dingam asked.

"Right-handed. What difference does that make? It's my leg that's hurt, not my hand."

Rosemary handed the doctor some peroxide and gauze

pads for sterilizing Bick's thigh. The doctor began wiping the area around the wound.

"What did you do with the cat?" Officer Dingam asked.

"What cat?"

"The one you stole from a backyard in Valley View Estates?"

"I don't know what you're talking about."

"I have a witness who saw you drive out of Valley View Estates with his family's pet cat in your truck. The cat was yowling and scratching at the window, trying to get out."

"The witness was mistaken. I didn't steal any cat."

"You didn't accidentally shoot yourself while putting away your gun, either," Officer Dingam said. "I can tell the bullet's angle from the wound. When the gun went off, it was held at shoulder height, aimed from right to left across your body. If you had been putting the gun in the holster when it fired, as you say you were, it would have been pointed straight down and you'd have held it much lower.

"Since you're right-handed," Officer Dingam continued, "the gun would have been in your right hand, and if it went off when you put it in the holster, the wound would have been in your right leg. Either someone else fired the gun or you were aiming it elsewhere when it went off."

Bick scowled and said nothing.

"Who were you aiming at?" Officer Dingam asked.

When Bick didn't reply, he said, "Maybe it was a person who scratched you. Who'd you fight with?"

"I was alone. There wasn't any other person."

"Then you must have been aiming at the cat," the officer said. "You were trying to shoot the cat, weren't you, the one you stole?"

"Why would I steal a cat? I don't even like cats. Snoopy creatures, always poking their noses where they don't belong."

The officer shrugged. "We already have a complaint against you for trespassing and theft. I can always add lying to an officer."

"Okay, okay," Bick said. "I got scratched and bit by a cat, but you can't pin any theft on me. I can't help it if a cat got in my truck and I didn't notice him until I was a few miles down the road."

Bick started to sit up, but the doctor said, "Lie still, please. I'm putting Novocaine in that wound so you'll be comfortable while I clean it." Bick lay back down, frowning.

Using cotton balls saturated with disinfectant, Rosemary began dabbing at the scratches on Bick's face. Bick winced, gritting his teeth. "You got no proof of trespassing or theft," Bick said. "You got no proof of anything."

"We have a witness who saw you drive off with his cat who was yowling and trying to get away, and you have multiple cat scratches and bite wounds. If the cat had been in your truck by accident, all you had to do was open the door and let him out."

Rosemary continued to clean the scratches.

Bick closed his eyes.

"Four people heard a gunshot," Officer Dingam said, "and saw your truck racing away from the area immediately afterward. They got the license number, then drove a short distance and saw blood on the side of the road. My department is checking that out as we speak. If you weren't shooting the cat, who were you shooting? Are you saying instead of theft, you could be held for attempted murder?"

"No! There wasn't anybody with me. You can't commit murder when you're alone!"

"If you were alone, then you're the one who pulled the trigger."

"That's right. I already told you that. I didn't shoot anyone else, and I didn't shoot a cat, either. I accidentally shot myself."

"Whose blood was on the side of the road?"

"Mine. From my leg."

"We can check that. DNA makes it easy to prove or disprove."

"So check it," Bick said. "It's my blood, all right."

"If nobody else was there, and the gun didn't discharge as you put it away, what did happen?" Officer Dingam asked.

"Maybe the cat shot him," Rosemary said.

The officer looked at the ceiling, as if to say, Oh, sure.

"Really. I read about a case where some guy was shooting a litter of puppies he didn't want and the last puppy struggled, and his paw hit the trigger. The guy's gun went off and he shot himself in the arm. The puppy got taken to a shelter, and dozens of people tried to adopt it. Too bad the man had already killed the other two puppies, or they would all have found good homes."

On the examining table, Bick squirmed, looking away from the officer.

"Don't move," the doctor said. "I'm putting on the dressing."

Officer Dingam said, "I suppose the cat could have done it, if he kicked hard enough and caught the trigger exactly right." He stared at the patient, waiting for him to deny that he'd been shot by a cat, but the man was silent, refusing to meet his eyes.

For a moment nobody spoke. Then the incredulous officer said, "That's what happened, isn't it? You were trying to shoot the cat, and somehow he got you instead."

"Stupid cat," Bick sputtered. "He fought like a wild tiger! I thought he was going to put my eye out with those claws. We struggled, and next thing I knew I heard the gun go off and felt the bullet hit my leg. His foot must have hit the trigger."

Rosemary swabbed disinfectant on the bite marks.

"Where's the cat now?" asked Officer Dingam.

"How would I know? I dropped him when the gun fired, and he took off, hightailed it into the woods with his fur puffed up like he'd stuck his tail in an electrical outlet. Last I saw him, he was streaking away faster than a shooting star. He's probably crossed the state line by now and is still running."

"Change Mr. Thorsen's chart, Nurse," the doctor said, "to show that the gunshot was inflicted by a cat."

It was all Rosemary could do not to laugh out loud.

"Perhaps you should change the name on the chart, too," the officer said. "I believe your patient is Bick Badgerton."

Bick's jaw dropped, but he did not deny the statement.

"Why didn't you tell the truth to begin with?" Officer Dingam asked. "You could have saved us a lot of time."

"Would you want to admit that a cat shot you in the leg?"

"No," the officer said, "I wouldn't. I'd never live it down."

"There you are," Bick said.

"All done," the doctor said as he removed his gloves. "I'm going to give you two prescriptions: one for antibiotics, and one for a painkiller. Take two pain pills tonight, and then one as needed." He wrote on a prescription pad, then tore the pages off and gave them to Bick.

Bick looked at the papers. "You got any free samples of these?" he asked. "I'm a little short of cash."

"I'm afraid not. You can try an over-the-counter pain-killer. It might be adequate. But you should take the antibiotics."

Bick gingerly swung his legs over the edge of the bed as he sat up.

"Call if you have any problems," the doctor said. "Otherwise come back tomorrow to get the dressing changed."

"I don't need to come back," Bick said. "I can change it myself."

Rosemary wanted to object, imagining this man with dirty fingernails removing the dressing, but she said nothing because she didn't want to intrude on the doctor's conversation.

"Clean those scratches on your face with hydrogen peroxide twice a day," the doctor said. "If you change your own dressing, sterilize your hands first."

Bick put his pants on, then started to untie the hospital gown.

Dr. Fleming turned to Rosemary. "You said the puppy who stepped on the trigger was adopted. What happened to the man who tried to shoot him?"

Rosemary finished writing on the chart. "He got arrested," she said, "and charged with animal cruelty."

"Funny," Officer Dingam said. "That's what's going to happen in this case, too."

"You can't prove a thing," Bick said. "Whatever I said here is confidential between me and my doctor. I was talking to him, not you."

"You deny that you tried to shoot that cat?" Officer Dingam asked.

"What cat?"

13

Alex fought back tears as he listened to his dad call the police. It seemed impossible that Pete had been taken away by the same man who had let Piccolo fall off the truck, but he knew that's what had happened. Benjie often made up wild stories about flying green panthers and other pretend creatures, but he would not have made up a story about Pete being kidnapped.

Benjie had seen Pete trying to get out of the man's truck, but what had happened after that? What did the man do to Pete up there in the woods, where he thought no one would see or hear him?

Oh, Pete, Alex thought. Where are you?

Mr. Kendrill hung up and said, "They'll let us know if they find Pete or the truck driver—but don't hold your breath. Although the man on the phone was sympathetic, it isn't realistic to think that the police will spend a lot of time looking for a lost cat."

"He isn't lost," Benjie said. "He's kidnapped."

"Can we go back up there and look for him?" Alex asked.

"It's awfully dark, son," Mr. Kendrill said, "and there are hundreds of acres of forest."

"I know, but we have to keep looking. He might be hurt, and I'm sure he's scared. We can't stay here and do nothing."

Mrs. Kendrill said, "We all need some dinner before we do anything else. Let's eat, and then decide."

Alex had no appetite, but he took a few bites of his grilled cheese sandwich and swallowed part of his tomato soup. Nobody talked during the meal.

When Alex carried his plate to the kitchen, Lizzy rubbed against his ankles. She wonders where Pete is, too, Alex thought. "Can we go back now and look some more?" he asked.

"Someone needs to stay here to answer the phone," Mr. Kendrill said. "The police will call if Pete's found, and our phone number is on Pete's collar, so we need to be here if someone finds him and calls. There's a chance that Pete got out of the truck before it ever left Valley View Estates, in which case he might find his way home. He could show up at the door."

"We heard the gunshot up in the woods," Alex said.

"Maybe he shot a bird. Maybe it was target practice."

Maybe, Alex thought, except target practice and bird hunting don't leave you with blood on your face.

"Benjie and I will stay here," Mrs. Kendrill said. "You and Alex go look in the woods some more."

"I want to help look," Benjie protested. "I don't want to stay here."

"If we haven't found Pete by tomorrow morning," Mrs. Kendrill said, "you can go and help search. For now we need to work in shifts."

Alex put on his denim jacket and his Seattle Mariners baseball cap. He put extra flashlight batteries in his pocket.

"Don't stay out too long," Mrs. Kendrill said. "And watch where you step. There's no telling how many traps are in that area."

Alex shuddered. He couldn't bear to think of Pete caught in one of those awful traps.

"We'll be careful," Mr. Kendrill said. "We'll stay together."

When they got to the third wide spot, where they'd found the drops of blood, Mr. Kendrill pulled over and they both got out of the car. Mr. Kendrill opened the trunk and removed the kerosene lantern that they used when they went camping. He lit the lantern and set it on top of the car. "To be sure we can find our way back," he explained. "It's mighty dark out here."

Alex nodded. He had never been afraid of the dark, but he had to admit he wouldn't want to be alone in this place at night. There were no streetlights, no houses, no cars on the road. It felt as if he were in one of those scary movies where he and his dad were the only two people on Earth.

His flashlight and his dad's flashlight made two bright pools of light on the ground. They agreed to walk straight into the woods, perpendicular to the car, on the theory that if Pete was running from Hogman, he would have run in as straight a line as possible. They stayed two car lengths apart, in order to search as much of the undergrowth as possible.

"Pete!" Alex called. "Here, Pete! Where are you?" Each time he called, he was quiet for a few seconds, hoping to hear Pete respond, but he heard only his dad's shoes on the forest floor.

He kept his flashlight pointed down, just ahead of him, and he kept his eyes down, too, mindful of the possibility of another trap. The darkness stretched ahead of him and closed behind him, as if he were a ship cutting through dark water.

Once, Alex thought he heard an animal sound, a meow perhaps, and he stopped walking. His dad must have heard it, too, because he stopped at the same time.

"Pete?" Alex called. He swept his light in an arc, searching. "Pete!"

A flapping sound came from partway up a tree a few feet in front of Alex, followed by a whoosh! He jerked his light upward in time to see a big brown bird flying away. Its wingspan must have been nearly three feet.

"Owl," Mr. Kendrill said.

Alex's pulse raced. He wondered if owls were carnivores. A bird that size would have sharp talons and a big beak. It would make short work of a cat.

Alex took a deep breath and tried to think of something else. He noticed that his dad's flashlight was moving up and down from tree to ground, as if he were riding a carousel horse. Dad's checking the tree branches as well as the ground, Alex realized, in case Pete had climbed a tree. He began swinging his flashlight up and down, too.

It was slow going. The farther they got from the road, the thicker the undergrowth was. There were decaying trees that had fallen in past storms, and large stumps left by long-ago loggers.

Every few minutes, they paused and looked back toward the car. The lantern was a faint glow in the distance now, and much smaller than it had been the first time they looked, but they could still see it.

"Pete! Here, Pete!" The dense woods seemed to swallow Alex's words. Even if Pete responded, Alex wasn't sure he'd hear the meowing of a cat unless he was right on top of him. He kept calling, though.

"I think we'd better turn back," Mr. Kendrill said. "The lantern's almost out of sight."

Fear clutched at Alex's throat. "We can't quit," he said. "After we get back to the car, let's try searching in a different direction."

"We can't stay out here all night," Mr. Kendrill said.

"No, but we could look on the other side of the road. We could go that way for as long as we can see the lantern."

"Let's move to our right a few feet, and then turn around," Mr. Kendrill suggested. "That way we aren't retracing the same path."

Alex headed to his right. He'd gone only a few feet when he heard the sound of branches breaking, followed by, "Oh!"

Alex spun around, shining his light toward the noise. At first he didn't see anything. "Dad?" he said.

"Over here."

Alex saw a faint light coming from the ground; he headed toward his dad's voice. His dad lay on his side, his eyes closed. The flashlight had fallen from his hand and now rested at the base of a tree, its light pointed downward.

Alex dropped to his knees beside his father. "Dad?" he said.

Mr. Kendrill moaned and opened his eyes. He started to sit up, then moaned again and put his head back down.

"What happened?" Alex said. "Are you okay?" He retrieved his dad's flashlight and handed it over.

"My leg," Mr. Kendrill said. "I think I may have broken my leg." He held the light at his waist and aimed it toward his shoes.

Alex gasped when he saw his dad's left pant leg bent at an odd angle.

"You'll have to go for help, son," Mr. Kendrill said. "I won't be able to walk out of here."

"Not even if I support you? You could put your arm around my shoulder and lean on me."

"That might work on a smooth surface," Mr. Kendrill said, "but not out here. You'll have to walk down the hill by yourself. If you can find a phone in Hilltop, call nine-one-one, and then call Mom. Otherwise, you'll have to walk all the way home."

"But I can't leave you here when you aren't able to walk," Alex said. "What if a bear comes along or a cougar?"

"Then you'll probably hear me yelling all the way into Valley View Estates." His voice got higher as he talked; the last word sounded as if it had been squeezed out, along with all Mr. Kendrill's breath. Although his dad was trying to joke, Alex could tell he was in serious pain.

"Should I try to put a splint on the leg before I leave? I learned how when I earned my Boy Scout first-aid badge."

"Good idea."

Alex found a tree branch, an inch in diameter and about six feet long, on the ground. He stripped it of all the leaves and small side branches, then put the middle of the branch on his knee and snapped the branch in half.

Kneeling beside his dad, he placed one piece of branch on each side of the leg. He hesitated. "This will hurt," he said. "Maybe I should wait until the medics come."

"No. Don't wait."

Alex put his hands gently on the broken leg. Gritting his teeth and hoping he was doing the right thing, he pushed the bottom of the leg until it lay straight.

Mr. Kendrill grunted a few times, and Alex could see his hands clenched into tight fists.

When the leg and the two pieces of branch were lined up parallel, like the stakes of a picket fence, Alex took off his jacket, removed his long-sleeved shirt, and sank his teeth into the top of one sleeve.

Keeping his teeth clamped shut, he yanked on the shirt until the sleeve tore off. Then he did the same thing with the other sleeve. Using the sleeves, he tied the two sticks tight against the pant leg, one directly below the knee and the other midway down his dad's calf.

"You okay?" he asked, when he had finished.

"Yes. It's better now that it's straightened out," Mr. Kendrill said. He was breathing hard and Alex saw him wipe the perspiration from his upper lip. He eased over onto his back, shifting his hips slightly but not moving the broken leg.

Alex put his sleeveless shirt back on, followed by his jacket.

"Go back toward the lantern light," Mr. Kendrill said.

"I could try to drive the car," Alex said. "I've watched you; I think I could do it, and I'd get down the hill a lot faster."

Mr. Kendrill shook his head. "Too risky," he said. "You'll have to walk. Go as fast as you can, but don't take any chances."

Alex nodded. He didn't want to leave his dad, but he knew he had to.

"I'm going to turn my flashlight off as soon as you're out of my sight," Mr. Kendrill said. "I'll save the battery until you come back with help. It'll be easier to find me if I have the light."

"I'll honk the horn when I get to the car," Alex said, "so you'll know I found the road."

Mr. Kendrill took the car keys from his pocket and handed them to Alex. "Be careful, son," he said. Then he closed his eyes, and Alex set off toward the car, walking as fast as he could through the dense, dark forest.

He continued to call, "Pete! Come here, Pete!" but he didn't stop to listen for a reply and he didn't take time to shine his light up into the trees. While he still feared for

Pete and wanted to look for him, he knew his first priority now was to get help for his dad.

What else can go wrong? Alex wondered.

Walking through underbrush was hard work. Alex had to lift his feet high with each step, as if he were a drum major. He kept the light pointed a few feet in front of him, looking before he took each step. Dad had proven how easy it was to trip and fall. Every few feet he glanced up long enough to be certain he was still headed for the lantern. Its light gradually grew brighter as he got closer.

By the time Alex reached the car, his legs were so tired that all he wanted to do was flop down on the backseat and take a nap.

Instead, he unlocked the car, reached in the door, and honked the horn: dum-da-da-dum-dum. It was the way his dad always knocked on Alex's bedroom door or on the bathroom door if Alex was taking too long in the shower.

He turned off the lantern, saving the kerosene for when he returned with help. For a moment he considered trying to drive the car, even though Dad had told him not to. He could sit behind the wheel, turn the key, put the engine in DRIVE and steer down the hill. He'd be home in ten minutes, rather than the thirty or forty it would take him to walk.

Alex knew that an automobile could be dangerous. People die in auto accidents every day. What if he took a curve too fast and ran off the road? What if he hit another car? What if a deer jumped out in front of him, and he couldn't stop? "Too risky," Dad had said, and Alex knew his dad was right.

He closed the car door, locked it, and started down the road.

Now that he was on gravel, he picked up the pace, alternating between jogging and a fast walk. He wondered how long it would take him to get home. He didn't have his watch on; he didn't know how long it had taken him to reach the car.

He thought back to the day they'd seen Piccolo fall off the truck. He and Rocky had run all the way home that day and had made it in only half an hour. But tonight Alex had already struggled through the woods until his legs were ready to collapse, and he had not yet even come to the place where they'd found the pig.

Don't think about how far it is, he told himself. Just put one foot in front of the other and keep going.

Dad's counting on me, he thought, and pushed himself to jog faster.

He had passed the second wide spot, where his family had pulled off to look for Pete, when he saw two round spots of light ahead. A car! A car was coming! Alex started to run. Maybe Mom had heard from the police. Maybe they'd found Pete and she was coming to tell him and Dad.

The lights grew bigger—and then Alex heard the engine noise. Dread took his breath away. It wasn't Mom; it was Hogman. By now, Alex knew that engine sound all too well. He turned and went into the woods beside the road, hoping that Hogman had not already seen him.

As soon as he reached a big tree, he crouched behind it and waited. The truck chugged closer. Was it slowing because the man had seen him or did it go slower because the hill got steeper here?

Alex stayed hidden. He could see the headlights and hear the rattling truck. He held his breath when the vehicle was directly opposite his hiding place, then slowly exhaled as Hogman continued on up the road. Then another thought froze him with fear. What would Hogman do when he saw the Kendrills' car parked on the side of the road?

What if he stopped? What if he could see the broken branches where Alex and his dad had walked? What if he followed their trail and found Dad, lying on the ground with a broken leg? Would he help Dad? More likely, he'd rob him, or ditch his old truck and steal the car. People like Hogman don't follow society's rules; they do what they want.

Alex hurried back to the road and raced downhill. As he ran he tried to convince himself that Hogman wouldn't bother to investigate the parked car. Hogman won't recognize our car, he thought. He won't know that the car has anything to do with his pig, or with the cat he kidnapped. He'll probably think the car was stolen and abandoned, and he won't even stop.

Alex's legs ached, and he could feel a blister starting on his left heel, but he kept running. He ran past where they'd gone into the woods and found the trap, and he ran past the first wide spot in the road. When he reached the edge of Hilltop, he paused to catch his breath.

He saw lights in a couple of windows down the street, and he wondered if he should knock on a door and ask for help. But he didn't know who lived there and he was uneasy about approaching a strange house at night. People get jittery. It would take him only another ten minutes to run the rest of the way home.

He took a deep breath, and kicked himself into high gear.

14

Pete held onto *the branch and thought about all the good things he would miss if he never found his way back home. Kitty num-num topped the list, followed closely by Alex's kitty massages. There was the sunny spot under the dining room table, and the c-a-t words in the dictionary, and the joy of catapulting to the top of the entertainment center. He had not yet had a chance to caterwaul and catapult for his family at the same time, and he had looked forward to performing that new trick.*

He would miss sitting on a lap while his family watched a movie, and he would miss eating some of their popcorn, even if they were a bit stingy about the amount they shared with him. He would miss his morning crunchies, and washing Lizzy's ears, and having a cat fit when the house got too quiet. He would even miss Benjie's spy games.

I should have stayed inside, Pete thought. I have a happy life with the Kendrills; I have food and a warm bed and peo-

ple who love me—why am I working so hard and taking such chances to prove that Hogman is trapping animals illegally? It's none of my business.

But even as he had that thought, Pete knew it wasn't true. The illegal trapping WAS his business. It was the business of everyone who cared about animals. I'm the one who saw the pelts, Pete thought. I'm the one who has the invoice hidden under a fern. If I don't stop him, who will?

He kidnapped me and tried to shoot me in the head. If he isn't stopped, he might do other terrible, unexpected things.

Pete wondered how someone like Hogman got to be the way he was. Hogman looked to be about the same age as Mr. Kendrill, but the two men were as different as sunshine and snow. Mr. Kendrill joked with his family, and was always kind to Pete and Lizzy. Even when he got cross with Pete for sneaking out the door, he only scolded; he never punished Pete.

"Oh, Pete," he would say when Pete had a cat fit or urped up a hair ball. "Stop acting like a cat!" He always smiled as he said it.

Hogman wore a perpetual scowl and sought revenge when Pete acted like a cat.

I need to get down out of this tree, Pete decided. I have to find my way home so I can show that invoice and the rabbit's foot to Alex. Slowly, Pete looked over his shoulder, gauging whether he could turn around on the branch or if he would have to back up until he reached the tree's trunk. There wasn't room to turn around; he would need to back up.

His stomach growled. He wished he'd eaten before he started out. How could he climb out of this tree when he was weak from hunger? He didn't like the idea of trying to get out of the tree in the dark, but if he waited until morning there would be nothing but a cat skeleton lying on this branch.

Pete raised himself slightly, until there was an inch of space between his tummy and the branch. Then, one paw at a time, he moved backward down the trunk of the tree. It was too dark to see the ground, which he knew was just as well. If he couldn't see how far down it was, he wouldn't be quite so nervous.

Rosemary had watched the patient limp down the hospital hall and enter the elevator. He had refused her offer of a wheelchair, which the hospital provided to all discharged patients to get them safely out the front door. He had refused a prescription for antibiotics, too, saying he couldn't afford them.

As the elevator doors closed behind him, she turned to Officer Dingam, who was still talking to Dr. Fleming.

"Can he get away with that?" she asked. "Can he admit to taking the cat and trying to kill it, and then walk away as if it never happened?"

"No," the officer said. "I don't normally follow up on a

missing animal, but I'll pursue this case. I might not be able to prove that he tried to shoot the cat, but I should be able to prove that he stole it. I don't have enough facts to charge him yet, though. I need to get statements from the cat's owners."

"If there's any way I can help, I'll be glad to do it," she said. "That guy was a slime bag." Realizing she was talking about a patient, Rosemary glanced quickly at Dr. Fleming.

Dr. Fleming only nodded his agreement, and picked up the next patient's chart.

Officer Dingam called headquarters from his patrol car. "I'm leaving the hospital," he told Sgt. Skyler. "The patient admitted he had the cat, although he claims he didn't take it on purpose. He tried to shoot it, but somehow the cat managed to hit the trigger with his paw and the man got shot in the leg."

He heard muffled laughter on the other end of the line. "If there's nothing urgent for me," he went on, "I'm going to have a chat with the cat's owners. Bick Badgerton dropped the cat after it shot him, and the cat ran off into the woods. Since the family knows approximately where that happened, they might be able to go there and find their pet."

Sgt. Skyler said, "Nothing much happening, for a change." He gave Officer Dingam the Kendrills' address. "Can you charge him with animal cruelty?"

"Not yet. Since the doctor was in the room when we

had the discussion, Badgerton claims he was talking to the doc and everything he said is confidential. That's another reason I want to talk to the cat's owners. If I can't nail this guy on cruelty, maybe I can get him on theft."

Mrs. Kendrill was home when Officer Dingam arrived. "My husband and my oldest son are up there now, looking for Pete," she said, after he had told her about his conversation at the hospital.

"I knew it!" Benjie said. "I knew Pete would shoot the meanie Hogman!"

Officer Dingam had Benjie tell him about seeing Pete in the truck. Then Mrs. Kendrill told about hearing the gun go off, and seeing the man speed away. They also filled him in on the pig situation and explained that this was the reason they recognized the truck.

Officer Dingam said, "The pig puts a new slant on all of this. I can charge him with transporting an animal in an unsafe manner."

After the police officer left, Mrs. Kendrill said, "Now that we know for sure that Pete is somewhere in the woods, we don't need to stay here to answer the phone. Let's go find Dad and Alex, and help them look for Pete."

As Mrs. Kendrill and Benjie drove out of Valley View Estates, they saw someone running down the road toward them.

"It's Alex!" Benjie cried.

Alex ran to the car. "Dad's hurt!" he said. "He broke his leg!"

Mrs. Kendrill went home, called 911, gave directions, and said she would meet the ambulance at the scene.

Ten minutes later, she parked behind her husband's car.

"He's that way," Alex said, pointing into the woods. "I'll honk the horn, to let him know we're here." Alex hit the horn, dum-da-da-dum-dum, as he had before. He got matches out of the glove compartment and relit the kerosene lantern, which still sat on the car roof.

"Benjie, you stay in the car and wait for the medics," Mrs. Kendrill said. "Alex is going to take me to Dad. When the medics come, honk the horn, then show them which way to go."

Benjie nodded.

Alex and his mother turned on their flashlights and started into the woods. Alex's legs ached from all the running; it hurt to lift his feet up high enough to walk back into the undergrowth, but he knew his pain was nothing compared to his dad's.

"Dad!" he called, over and over. "Where are you?"

"Are you sure this is the right way?"

"Yes." Alex thought he was headed in the right direction, but it was hard to be positive in the dark. "Dad!" he called again.

A faint glimmer of light appeared through the trees. "There!" Alex said. "That must be his flashlight!"

Alex and his mom walked faster; the light grew brighter.

"We're coming, Dad!" Alex called. "We see your light!"

They found him on the ground, in exactly the same position he'd been in when Alex left. He smiled weakly. "Good job, son," he said. "I knew you could do it."

"The medics are on their way," Mrs. Kendrill said. "Benjie's in the car, waiting for them."

"I'll go partway back," Alex said, "so they can see my flashlight and get here quickly."

He started toward the car and soon heard the horn and saw a flashing blue light. "This way!" he called, waving his flashlight back and forth. Two men carrying a stretcher and other supplies came toward him through the trees with Benjie trailing behind them. Alex led them to his dad.

While they checked Mr. Kendrill, Alex took off his jacket and placed it on the ground a short distance from where his dad was. "I'm leaving my jacket here," he told Benjie. "Cats have a good sense of smell. If Pete comes this way, maybe he will recognize my scent and stay nearby."

As his dad was safely loaded into the ambulance, Alex's mother told the medics, "We'll follow you to the hospital."

"What about Pete?" Alex asked. "Maybe I should stay here and look some more."

"I could stay, too," Benjie said. "I can help find Pete."

"Pete will have to wait until tomorrow," Mrs. Kendrill said. "I don't want you boys out here by yourselves at night, with no way to get home."

Alex hated the thought of Pete spending the rest of the night lost in the woods, but he knew his mom was right. He was too tired to search properly, and he certainly didn't have the energy to walk all the way back home again. He got into the car, followed by Benjie.

When they arrived at the hospital, Mr. Kendrill was taken to have his leg X-rayed while Mrs. Kendrill filled out the paperwork. Half an hour later, Rosemary met the whole family in an emergency-room cubicle and told them that Mr. Kendrill's leg was definitely broken.

"How did it happen?" she asked.

"My son and I were out in the woods looking for our cat," Mr. Kendrill said.

Before he could continue, Rosemary interrupted. "The cat that got kidnapped?" she asked.

"Yes," Alex said. "How do you know about Pete?"

"I helped treat the man who accidentally got shot," she said. "I'm the one who called the police."

"Thank you," Mrs. Kendrill said. "Officer Dingam came to our house after he left the hospital."

"He did?" Alex said.

"He's looking for evidence to charge Hogman with stealing Pete," Benjie said.

Dr. Fleming came then and explained that he would need to set the leg and put a cast on it. "We'll keep you overnight," he told Mr. Kendrill, "but you will probably be able to go home tomorrow. No walking in the woods for a while, though."

"These are the cat owners," Rosemary told him. "That's why Mr. Kendrill was in the woods at night; he was looking for Pete."

"I hope you find him," Dr. Fleming said. "By the way, that splint made out of branches was a clever idea, and helped stabilize the leg while you were being transported."

Alex smiled. It was good to know that one thing had gone right.

The smile didn't last long. Talk of Pete made all of Alex's fears rise up from the back of his mind, where he had pushed them while he ran for help. He was relieved that Dad was going to be okay, but by helping Dad he had abandoned the search for Pete. Now his imagination filled with all the potential tragedies that could befall a cat in the deep woods at night.

15

Officer Dingam and Sgt. Skyler stared glumly into their coffee mugs. "I can't arrest him for taking the cat," Officer Dingam said, "or for trying to shoot it. There isn't enough evidence to make a case."

"What about the pig?"

"That case is dicey, too. If I pursue it and some hotshot attorney gets him off, Badgerton would get the pig back. Then those kids would have lost their cat and their pig. I'm not sure it's worth taking the chance."

"Where's a bum like Badgerton going to come up with money for a hotshot attorney?"

"You never know. He might have a rich uncle."

"Does he have a job? How does he support himself?"

"He wrote 'self-employed farmer' on the hospital information sheet, but that doesn't mean anything. He put a fictitious name and address, too."

"Sounds as if he has something to hide."

"Yes. But what is it?"

. . .

I'm lost, Pete thought. He had made it down out of the tall tree, but now that he was on the ground, he had no idea which way he should go. He looked around. Every direction he looked, he saw nothing but trees.

Pete shivered but not from the cold. His beautiful brown-and-white fur coat kept him warm enough. He shivered at the idea that he might never find his way home. He might never see Alex again and eat kitty num-num and get a kitty massage. He might never get to catapult and caterwaul at the same time.

Pete sat at the base of the tree and tried to make a plan. He was a clever, courageous, and capable cat who had helped his family many times. Now he needed to figure out a way to help himself.

I would be able to think better if I wasn't hungry, Pete decided. He sat as still as a stone, listening. Before long he heard a slight scurrying sound from under a nearby bush. Pete crept closer to the sound, his whiskers twitching as he smelled a mouse.

The sound stopped. Pete crouched beside the bush and waited, staring at the base of the bush. Soon the scurrying started again, and when a plump mouse poked its head out from under the bush, Pete pounced.

A few minutes later, as he washed his paws and whiskers, Pete wondered why the cat food companies only offered flavors such as "salmon" and "chicken." Any cat could tell them "mouse" cat food would be an instant hit.

With his stomach pleasantly full, Pete decided on a plan. He would walk in one direction, stopping every few feet to scratch in the dirt or on a tree trunk. That way, if he didn't come to the road, he would be able to retrace his steps by watching for his scratch marks. Then he would try going in a different direction.

Pleased with his cleverness, he decided not to put the plan in motion right away. He needed a nap first. Running away from a cat murderer was tiring. Pete curled into a tight ball at the base of the fir tree, and fell asleep.

A loud flapping sound woke him. Instinctively, Pete leaped away. A sharp pain speared his shoulder and he felt a breeze in his face. Pete was raised up off the ground, his legs dangling, as if he were flying.

An owl! A huge owl had one talon hooked in Pete's shoulder and was lifting him upward. If he had not tried to jump aside when he woke up, the owl would have both talons embedded in Pete's back. Pete let out a caterwaul so loud that it hurt his own ears. At the same time he twisted around, trying to get free.

The owl screeched. It flew higher, with Pete suspended from one of its talons.

Pete was heavier than the owl's usual prey of field mice and voles; the owl struggled to fly high enough to clear the trees. As it came to a tall fir tree, Pete quit struggling and reached downward, grabbing a thick branch. He dug his claws in, as the owl cried out. For a moment Pete thought he would have to let go of the branch or have a chunk of his shoulder torn out, but the owl loosened its grip and flew away, complaining loudly.

Pete clung to the branch, fearing that the owl would circle around and try again. If the big bird got him with both talons, Pete knew he'd never get away.

When the owl did not return, Pete tried to lick the wound on his shoulder, but, although he could twist his head far enough to smell his own blood, he couldn't reach the injury with his tongue. I need to go home, Pete thought, and have my family take care of me. He moved slowly along the branch until he reached the trunk of the tree, then slid down.

When he reached the ground and tried to walk, he knew he was in big trouble. Each time he moved his right front foot, pain sliced through his shoulder. Every leaf or branch that grazed his back caused his wound to throb.

He couldn't walk all the way home. He'd never make it. He would have to find a hiding place, a safe spot where an owl couldn't swoop down on him. He would hide and wait for Alex to find him.

Keeping his eyes and ears alert for the owl or other predators, Pete limped toward where he thought the road was. He watched for a place to hide until morning, but found nothing. After a while, the shoulder pain settled into a steady ache. Pete kept going. *If I make it home,* he promised himself, *I will never, ever leave the house again.*

"Who—who—who."

Pete froze when he heard the owl's call ahead of him. Soon he heard an answering call and then the sound of wings flapping as the closer owl flew away.

Pete altered his course, veering to his right, away from the direction the owl had gone.

Just when he thought he was too tired to lift his paws one more time, he smelled something familiar. Pete sniffed. His heart quickened as he recognized Alex's scent. He wanted to call Alex's name, but he was afraid of making any sound, for fear that the owl would hear him and attack again.

Instead, Pete walked toward the smell, hoping, hoping.

The scent grew stronger, but Pete heard no humans in the woods. Unlike cats, people make sounds when they walk, even when they're trying to be quiet. Pete heard no leaves crunching, no twigs breaking, but he was certain he smelled Alex and soon he also smelled Mr. and Mrs. Kendrill and Benjie and other humans he didn't recognize.

His family had been here, in the woods, and he had missed them. *They probably came looking for me,* he thought. He sniffed all around, wondering what had happened in this place, and who the other people were.

Then he spotted Alex's jacket. Pete rubbed his face against it, inhaling the strong scent of Alex. *This will be my hiding place, he decided. I will be safe if I stay underneath Alex's jacket.*

He pawed at the jacket, which Alex had folded, until it made a heap on the ground. Then he put his head down, and crawled underneath it, making sure the jacket covered him completely. Satisfied that none of his fur showed, Pete lay on the ground beneath the jacket and fell asleep.

The grandfather clock in the hall was striking one A.M. when Alex, his mom, and Benjie finally got home. Benjie had fallen asleep in the car, so Alex helped him stagger into the house.

They had stayed at the hospital until Alex's dad had the cast on his leg and was drowsy from the pain medicine he'd been given.

Alex was half asleep himself. What a day! He turned down his mom's offer of some hot chocolate and slid between the sheets.

Most nights, as soon as Alex turned out the light, Pete would jump on the bed, purring and rubbing against Alex. He would climb on Alex's legs and settle himself there, stretched out with his head toward Alex's feet. Pete would sleep on Alex's legs all night if Alex would let him, but after ten or fifteen minutes, Alex always had to shift position, and Pete would slide off.

Now, alone in the bed, Alex couldn't fall asleep. He lay

there, missing Pete and worrying. Despite Pete's size and his noisy ways, Pete was a big softie. Except for leaping to the top of the entertainment unit and an occasional cat fit, Pete mostly slept, ate, and purred. He loved to sit in Alex's lap and get petted and although he sneaked outside frequently, he rarely left his own yard. Alex thought Pete went out mainly because he was curious about what the people were doing and wanted to be in on it, not because he had a desire for outdoor exercise.

Pete won't be able to defend himself if a coyote or other wild animal attacks him, Alex thought as his worry ripened into panic.

If I find him, Alex decided, he's going to be an indoor cat from now on, and this time I'll enforce the rule. I'll take him out on his leash so he can eat grass, and I'll throw his ball for him in the house, and I'll drag a long piece of string around so he can attack it. If I keep him entertained, he won't want to bolt out the door all the time.

First I have to find him.

Alex got out of bed, went downstairs, and opened the kitchen door, in case Pete had come home. In his imagination he could see Pete sitting in the grass at the foot of the steps, yowling at Alex and trying to get Alex to chase him.

He closed the door and went back to bed.

Eventually, Alex slept, but he woke early and his first thought was, "Pete's lost. I have to find Pete."

Mrs. Kendrill was in the kitchen making coffee when Alex went downstairs. "I'm going over to the hospital soon," she said. "Do you want to come along?"

"I'm going to look for Pete."

"I don't want you out in the woods by yourself. It isn't safe."

"Benjie can go with me."

"I know you're worried about Pete," Mrs. Kendrill said. "So am I. But you'll have to wait until later today, when I can go with you."

"Maybe Rocky and Mary can go with me now," Alex said. "You could drive us up the hill before you go to the hospital."

"It's too early to call them. They're probably still sleeping."

Alex looked at the clock. Seven thirty was earlier than he would normally call anyone, but this was an emergency and he was sure his friends wouldn't mind.

"They won't care if I wake them up," Alex said. "Not for something like this. If Rufus was missing, I'd help Rocky look for him, no matter what time it was. Remember when Pearly the possum was loose, and I helped Mary find her in the middle of the night? When someone needs help, their friends understand."

Mrs. Kendrill thought a second, then said, "You're right. Go ahead and call."

The plans were quickly made and half an hour later, Mary and Rocky arrived. Mrs. Sunburg came, too. She had offered to stay at the Kendrills' house so Mrs. Kendrill didn't have to wake up Benjie. She said she and Benjie would drive up the hill in two hours, to make sure the searchers were okay and to give them a ride home if they wanted to return.

"I brought whistles," Mary said, handing one to Alex and one to Rocky. "If we're separated, and you need help, blow the whistle."

By eight fifteen, Alex, Mary, and Rocky were standing by the bloodstains on the side of the road, watching Mrs. Kendrill's car go back down the hill toward the hospital.

"Dad and I went this way last night," Alex said, pointing.

"Then we should probably go the opposite direction now," Rocky said.

"I don't think it matters," Mary said. "Pete probably kept moving. Even if you looked in one area last night, that doesn't mean he isn't there now."

"I think we should search on the other side of the road today," Alex said, "but I left my jacket here last night, and I'm going to go get it first. It looks like rain, and I may need it."

"I'll start looking across the road," Rocky said.

"I'll go a little farther uphill," Mary said. "Blow your

whistle every ten minutes, so we keep track of each other. One toot means you're okay; more than one means come right away."

Alex started into the woods. It looked different in the daylight, less threatening. It was hard walking, though, because his whole body was stiff from the night before. Twice he heard Mary and Rocky blow a quick *tweet* on their whistles, and he blew his in reply. The second time, the whistles sounded far away.

It took him half an hour to find the place where his dad had fallen. He spotted his jacket, but it was not the way he had left it. He had folded it and laid it down; now it was crumpled in a heap.

Alex picked the jacket up and looked closely at it. There was cat hair on it—white-and-brown cat hair, Pete hair—but it could have been there all along. Lots of Alex's clothes were unintentionally decorated with Pete fur. He looked again. Two small spots stained the jacket lining, dark red spots. Bloodstains.

"Pete!" Alex shouted. "Pete, where are you? Here, kitty, kitty!" He took the whistle out of his pocket and blew it sharply three times. Pete had been here! Alex was sure of it. Pete had found the jacket and lain on it, maybe slept on it.

The bloodstains gave urgency to the search. Alex's hands felt clammy and the Cocoa Puffs he'd had for breakfast threatened to reappear. He blew three more sharp blasts on his whistle.

"Pete! Here, Pete!"

Tears stung Alex's eyes as he plunged deeper into the forest, away from the road. All he could think was: Pete is hurt, and I have to find him.

Pete had finished his breakfast mouse and was washing his face when he heard Alex's whistle.

What kind of bird is that? Pete wondered. It was a harsh sound, and Pete looked anxiously around, fearing another owl attack.

His shoulder throbbed this morning. It had taken all his determination to pounce on that mouse because he knew the jump would hurt, but it was either catch his own breakfast or go hungry. Pete believed a hearty breakfast was important. Also a tasty lunch, a dinner of kitty num-num, and several snacks in between.

With his stomach full of mouse, Pete washed his paws and whiskers. As soon as he was clean, he planned to return to Alex's jacket for a nap.

He heard the sharp "tweet" sound again. This time, he also heard Alex calling his name! Pete stood and limped toward the sound. "Here I am!" he cried. "Come and get me!"

Alex stopped. A tingle of excitement zapped from the back of his neck down both arms and legs. "Pete?" he called again. "Is that you?"

Pete thought, *Now would be a good time for me to cater-waul.* He took a deep breath, threw his head back, and let out the most shrill, harsh howl he could manage.

Seconds later, Alex spotted white fur ahead. He ran to Pete and scooped him up.

"Oh, Pete," Alex said. "I'm so glad to see you."

"What took you so long?" asked Pete.

16

Alex, still holding Pete, sat cross-legged on the side of the road beside Rocky and Mary, waiting for Mrs. Sunburg to arrive to give them a ride home. The sun felt warm on his back, and Pete was warm against his chest. I'm lucky, Alex thought. I'm incredibly lucky to have my cat back.

Instead of Mrs. Sunburg, Alex's mom drove up to the meeting place, with Benjie in the backseat.

Benjie jumped out of the car before it came to a complete stop. "You found him!" he said. "You found Pete!"

"Actually, I found Alex," Pete said. "I discovered his jacket and had the good sense to stay near it until he came back."

"He's hurt," Alex said. "I think he'll need to go to the vet."

"No!" Pete said. "Not the vet! I don't need to go to the vet. I refuse! All I need is some kitty num-num and a nap under the table."

Mrs. Kendrill examined the wound on Pete's back. "He may not need the vet," she said. "I can clean that up. It looks to me like Pete tangled with a hawk or some other big bird."

"How's Dad?" Alex asked.

"He's home. He was ready to be discharged when I got to the hospital."

They piled in the car and drove back to Valley View Estates.

"Why didn't you wake me up this morning?" Benjie complained. "I wanted to help look for Pete."

"You can help take care of him when we get home," Alex said. "He'll probably want some kitty num-num."

Pete sighed. Less than one minute ago, he had told Alex he wanted some kitty num-num, and now Alex said "probably" as if he hadn't heard a word Pete said.

Mrs. Kendrill started down the driveway.

"Oh, oh," Mary said. "Look who's at my house."

The old black pickup truck, with the door open, was backed up to the pigpen.

"It's Hogman," Benjie said. "He's in the pen with Piccolo!"

"He cut the wire!" Mary said.

"Everyone come inside with me," Mrs. Kendrill said. "I'll call your gramma, Mary, and find out what's going on."

Pete glared across the yard at the man in the pigpen. A

deep growl rumbled from his throat. "He tried to kill me," Pete said. "He killed lots of other animals, too, and sold their pelts."

"Shh, Pete," Alex said. "We won't let him get you."

"I have proof!" Pete said. "Put me down, and I'll show it to you."

A police car pulled into the Sunburgs' driveway, and stopped beside the truck. Officer Dingam got out, then walked toward the pigpen as Mrs. Sunburg hurried from the house.

"Gramma must have called the police," Mary said.

"It's the officer who came and questioned us about Pete," Mrs. Kendrill said.

"Let's go over there," Benjie said. "He might need our help."

"Hold my hand, Benjie," Mrs. Kendrill said, "and don't say anything."

"I'll put Pete inside," Alex said.

"Oh, no, you won't," Pete said. "I have something important to show you first."

"Hold still, Pete!" Alex said. "You can't get down now." He tightened his grip on the struggling cat. "What's the matter with you?" he said. "You need to go inside and stay there."

Across the yard, he heard the police officer say, "Bick Badgerton! What do you think you're doing with that pig?"

"I'm taking her home," Bick said. "She belongs to me."

"If she belongs to you, how'd she get here?"

"They stole her. Took her off the side of the road before I could get there to pick her up."

"I heard she fell off your truck."

"Well, now she's going back on it," Bick said.

Pete didn't want to scratch Alex, but he couldn't allow himself to be carried into the house. Not now, when the trapper was standing right there, talking to a police officer.

Pete thrust his hind feet against Alex's arm.

"Ouch!" Alex said, and loosened his grip.

Pete leaped to the ground and raced toward the clump of ferns.

"Get back here," Alex said. "Haven't you had enough excitement? You're lucky to be alive."

"This way!" Pete said. "Follow me!"

Even though it made his shoulder hurt more, Pete ran toward where he'd left the rabbit's foot and the invoice. This time, Alex ran after him.

Pete got there first and picked up the invoice in his teeth. Alex rushed to him, leaned down to pick him up, and stopped. "What's that?" he asked. "What do you have in your mouth?"

Pete dropped the invoice, and Alex picked it up. While Alex read it, Pete batted the rabbit's foot out from under the fern. Alex looked down, then picked up the rabbit's foot, too.

"Where did you get these?" Alex said. "I need to show these to the policeman."

Finally! Pete thought. He let Alex pick him up, but when Alex started toward his own house, Pete struggled again.

"Oh, all right," Alex said. "You can come along while I talk to the police officer, but you can't get down."

"I don't want to get down," Pete said. "I only want to hear what's said."

Alex ran toward the others. "Look what Pete found!" he said. He handed the invoice and the rabbit's foot to Officer Dingam.

"Where did you get these?" the officer said.

"My cat had them," Alex said. "He must have taken them out of the truck."

"That's probably why Hogman got angry and stole Pete," Benjie said.

"Hush, Benjie," Mrs. Kendrill said.

Officer Dingam said, "You're under arrest, Badgerton, for illegal trapping and sale of wildlife."

"You can't prove that," Bick said.

"I can!" Benjie said. "I have DNA evidence on a cigarette butt."

"Hush, Benjie," Mrs. Kendrill said.

Officer Dingam put the invoice in his pocket. "This invoice has your name on it," he said. "Get in the squad car. We're taking a trip to the station."

• • •

That night after dinner, everyone gathered at the Kendrills' house for ice cream. Mr. Kendrill sat with his leg propped up on a stool.

Pete sat by Alex's feet, hoping he would get to lick the bowl when Alex finished eating. He had reminded the people that cats like dessert, too, but as usual, the humans had not done what he asked.

"Officer Dingam called," Alex said. "He found six more leghold traps, all of them set, around the trailer where Hogman was living, and the fingerprints on them matched Hogman's. He said there's plenty of evidence to convict the man on animal cruelty, which is a felony, and he'll ask that part of the sentence be that Hogman can't own any animal for at least three years."

"Humans don't own animals," Pete said. "You merely take care of them."

"That means Piccolo gets to stay with us," Mary said.

Benjie cheered. Rocky gave the thumbs-up sign.

Maybe it won't be so bad, Pete thought. If Piccolo is as smart as the people claim she is, she might make an interesting friend. Pete liked Lizzy, but she couldn't discuss current events, and when Pete had asked her opinion about who would win the World Series, Lizzy had no idea what he was talking about.

Tomorrow Pete would sneak out and pay that pig a visit.

If Piccolo didn't understand Cat, perhaps Pete could learn to speak Pig. Maybe pig language would have some new words that start with c-a-t.

"Officer Dingam also told us to watch the news on channel four at six-thirty," Alex said. "That's why we invited you to come over now." He turned on the television.

Partway through the broadcast, the station played the brief clip of Bick Badgerton covering his face as he hurried to his truck.

The reporter, Jenna Martinez, said, "Hilltop Police have made an arrest for a bank robbery that was committed seven years ago. Channel four has this exclusive picture of the suspect."

"I knew it," Benjie said. "I knew Hogman was hiding from the law!"

"Hush, Benjie," Mrs. Kendrill said.

"The suspect lives in the woods west of Hilltop in an abandoned trailer that was once used as a temporary office for a timber company," Jenna said. "Police had charged him with illegal trapping and animal cruelty, but when they ran his fingerprints through the computer, the prints matched those of a man wanted for bank robbery."

Officer Dingam appeared on the TV screen. "When the bank was robbed," he said, "two citizens gave chase. The robber dropped the bag of money when he ran away, so the fingerprints from that bag were on file."

Jenna Martinez returned. "Mr. Badgerton will be arraigned in court next Thursday," she said as the clip of Hogman with his hands over his face ran again. "Stay tuned to channel four for updates."

A commercial came on, and Alex turned the TV off.

"Wow!" Rocky said. "We not only helped nab a trapper, we caught a bank robber!"

"*Who caught the trapper?*" Pete asked. "*Who found the evidence? I'm the hero! I'm the one who should have been interviewed.*"

"Do you think Pete's shoulder hurts?" Mr. Kendrill asked. "Is that why he's yowling?"

"Maybe we had better take him to the vet in the morning, after all," Mrs. Kendrill said.

"*No!*" Pete said. "*He would take my temperature and make unflattering remarks about my size. I won't go!*" He *growled while his tail swished back and forth on the carpet.*

Mary opened a large bag that she had brought along. "In all the excitement of getting Pete back and seeing Hogman arrested," she said, "I forgot to show you what I found yesterday." She removed a deer antler.

"Where did you find that?" Alex asked.

"I looked for Pete while you were at the hospital. When I went in the trees behind Elm Lane, it was lying on the ground, and I picked it up."

Alex groaned. The antler had been practically in his own backyard.

"Do you want me to sell it for you on eBay?" Rocky said.

"No. I'm going to hang it in my room."

Pete stood up and walked from Alex to Benjie, politely asking for his own dish of ice cream.

"He moves okay," Mr. Kendrill said. "Maybe he's yowling because he's hungry."

"I'll feed him as soon as I finish my ice cream," Alex said.

Pete looked at all the humans, comfortable and relaxed as they ate their ice cream. Pete thought this would be a fine opportunity to catapult and caterwaul at the same time. But first, he needed to get rid of a hair ball. With all the mouse fur he had swallowed recently, he was sure he could bring up an especially big one. He stood in the center of the room, stuck out his tongue, and began to retch.

A NOTE FROM PEG KEHRET:

For those who want to learn more about pigs, I recommend *The Whole Hog: Exploring the Extraordinary Potential of Pigs* by Lyall Watson. Smithsonian Books, 2004

The idea of a pig who fell from a truck on her way to be slaughtered came from an actual pig who jumped onto a busy highway and was lucky enough to be rescued by Pasado's Safe Haven. The incident of the puppy shooting a man who was trying to kill him is also based on fact.

Trapping laws vary from state to state. While it is true that many countries have banned leghold traps, some states in the United States still allow them.

A NOTE FROM PETE THE CAT:

I'm too tired to write any more. If you have questions, you'll find me under the table in the sunny spot, washing Lizzy's ears.

03 07.